Praise for *Kingpin and Eli:*

"Broadcast veteran and management mentor, Buck Dopp has all the goods: a record of excellence, and a love for the business. The latter is the nerve center of his first novel. With unforgettable characters, Buck brings us the morality conflicts that play out in so many American newsrooms. It was a pleasure to work with him, and to celebrate his author debut."

—Larry Kane, 45 year veteran TV news anchor and author of *When They Were Boys*

"Kingpin wears the power gained by stepping on other people like the crown of an anointed king. But what happens to the popular and visible TV station anchor when that crown is threatened? Murder? Would Kingpin resort to that? The reader will follow the twisting trail of fall and redemption with Kingpin and his ally the mysterious Eli. With a skill born of the love and acute understanding of people, Buck Dopp creates a flawed, but lovable, cast of characters who influence, support and enliven Kingpin's journey for better and for worse. These characters are so real the reader will be sure that he or she knows them and only their names have been changed."

—Patricia Agnew, author of *How to Talk to Your Doctor.*

"Anyone who's ever worked in a major newsroom will be wondering, 'is the author talking about my workplace?'"

—Kevin Walsh, author of *The Perfect Catch*

"I had the pleasure of working with Buck for several years. He is a very skilled leader who always manages his areas of responsibility with great effectiveness. Buck managed both business units and studio locations during his tenure at CN8, The Comcast Network, and always achieved and exceeded budgeted objectives. He is an excellent communicator, problem solver, and idea generator, and works well as both a leader, and as part of a senior management team."

—Jon Gorchow, President of Lenfest Broadcasting

"I have known this man and his family for over 20 years. Buck understands people and has a common sense approach to problems that makes complex things seem simple. He is an inspirational leader who knows his people so well and gets the most out of them. He understands the bottom line and he also understands how to make people happy. His leadership qualities are unique and his passion for people is rare."

—Michael Doyle, Senior Vice President Video & Operations at Rogers Communications

"Buck Dopp's writing is consistently a joy to read. He tells a story with clarity, wit and intensity; his work is technically proficient, and his style is gripping and passionate. He also has excellent managerial skills, is reliable and conscientious, ethical and personable. Working with Buck has always been a rewarding, enjoyable experience for me."

—Gabrielle Sinclair, writer/actress

"Buck Dopp is a dedicated leader with strong writing and critiquing skills. Under Buck's leadership, the Lake Havasu City Writers Group flourished. Buck's writing contains wonderful elements such as humor, well drawn characters, and stories that compel the reader forward."

—Paul L. Bailey, president of the Lake Havasu City Writers Group and author of *Fate's Knight*

"Buck Dopp is a talented, eclectic writer whose talents cross a wide menagerie of genres. Though some of his subjects might be quite serious, his style lends an air of tongue-in-cheek humor to most of his work. Buck's work is always readable and always enjoyable, often with that perfect "Ah-ha" moment for the reader when a plot turn is finally revealed. In addition to his smooth writing skills, Buck is also an excellent hands-on manager, assuming the role of President of his writers group and leading it into new directions and encouraging people to think outside of their restrictive boxes.

He does this by the strength of his personality, leading rather than pushing and always with a smile and an upbeat attitude."

—Jim Veary, writer and past president of the Lake Havasu City Writers Group

"I would like to recommend Buck Dopp as a writer and photographer. His work is thoughtful, professional, and entertaining. Buck is also a diligent writer whose final product always shows his dedication to craft."

—Cindie Miller, MFA, teacher and author of *Ask Me No Questions*

"Talented and hard-working, his stories are wonderful and I highly recommend him to anyone who likes a good story."

—EV Medina, author of *Realmwalkers*

"Buck Dopp is a talented writer with the knowledge of all the essentials of writing."

—Kelley Heckart, editor and author, *Of Water and Dragons*

"I've had the pleasure of knowing Buck Dopp for a few years now as a member of our local writer's group and as its president. He motivates others with his drive to keep improving his writing skills and his support of others who are doing the same. His critiques of his peers are always spot on with notes about what could make the piece better and what the writer did well."

—Sharon Poppen, author of *After the War Before the Peace*

"I have enjoyed reading the stories that Buck Dopp has sent to *Long Story Short's e-zine*, where I am assistant editor. He's easy to work with and a great addition to our published writers."

—Linda Barnett-Johnson, editor, proofreader and virtual assistant

Kingpin and Eli

A NOVEL

by

Buck Dopp

ISBN: 0615895301
ISBN-13: 9780615895307
Library of Congress Control Number: 2013919485
CreateSpace Independent Publishing Platform
North Charleston, South Carolina

TABLE OF CONTENTS

About the Author		ix
Acknowledgments		xiii
Introduction		xv
Prologue	Briggs Lake, Arizona	xvii
Chapter 1	Setting the Trap	1
Chapter 2	Witness to Murder	19
Chapter 3	Game Changer	27
Chapter 4	Takedown	37
Chapter 5	Kingpin Sees the Light	45
Chapter 6	Jocko Hires the Next Rising Star	61
Chapter 7	Another Chance	77
Chapter 8	Chicken Noodle Soup	91
Chapter 9	Pickler Probed	109
Chapter 10	Interviews	113
Chapter 11	Helping Others	119
Chapter 12	Fannie Ambushes Rump	129
Chapter 13	Baptism Brunch	133
Chapter 14	Journey to the Past	137
Chapter 15	Kingpin Returns	147
Chapter 16	Carmaletta's Miracle	163
Chapter 17	Project Hope	169
Chapter 18	Carmaletta Gets a Job	171
Chapter 19	Kingpin's Life Changes Again	173

Chapter 20   Killer Revealed   181
Chapter 21   Unfinished Business   189
Chapter 22   Case Closed   193
Epilogue   Coffee Time   199

ABOUT THE AUTHOR

Buck Dopp retired from a 27-year career in business management in 2008, deciding instead to write full-time. Dopp works as a free-lance writer for the *Today's News-Herald* in Lake Havasu City, Arizona. His short stories have appeared in *The Oasis Journal* and *Long Story Short's* e-zine. He is the past president of the Lake Havasu City Writers Group, which has published his stories in its anthology, *Offerings from the Oasis. Kingpin and Eli* is his first novel.

Dopp, born in Des Moines, Iowa, majored in English at Saint John's University in Minnesota before moving to California. It's there that he met his future wife Stephanie, whom he married in 1973 and with whom he raised four children. They live in Lake Havasu City, AZ, and have been married for forty years. Visit the author's website at www.buckdopp.com.

This book is dedicated to the love of my life and best friend, Stephanie, as we celebrate our fortieth wedding anniversary. Your support, guidance, and love continue to inspire my writing and everything else in my life. You are my muse and without your love I would never have become the man I am today. Thank you for everything.

ACKNOWLEDGMENTS

My deepest gratitude goes to the Lake Havasu City Writers Group, whose critiques of the early drafts have been invaluable and without whose support *Kingpin and Eli* would never have been written.

The back cover photograph was taken by my good friend Barry Morgenstein who is the best head-shot photographer I know. Visit his website at www.barrymorgenstein.com.

I give special thanks to my friends who read early drafts and whose questions and comments helped make the final version stronger: Pat and Jo Conmy, Don and Kathryn Johnson, Kert and Ruth Marty, Phil and Sue Wallace, Sally McClure, and Carol Romain.

INTRODUCTION

I've seen a lot during nearly three decades as a business leader. When we go to work we frequently face moral dilemmas as we strive to achieve our goals, company objectives, and help the coworkers on our team succeed. *Kingpin and Eli* is a story that aims to explore the choices real people make when facing moral conflicts. Sometimes we get it right and sometimes we don't. I've always wanted to write a novel that would be fast-paced, entertaining, and humorous, while giving the reader some food for thought. More than anything, I hope you have as much fun reading *Kingpin and Eli* as I did writing it.

Buck Dopp
Lake Havasu City, Arizona

Prologue

BRIGGS LAKE, ARIZONA

A taxi rolled up to the curb at the entrance of the Briggs News 20's TV station, interrupting the thoughts of a man clad in a t-shirt and jeans who had been scanning the sky for emerging stars while inhaling the cool April evening air. He opened the rear door and jumped in.

"Where to?" the driver asked.

"Just drive, dude."

"Sure thing. I'm Manny."

The man tossed a folder on the seat next to him. "So, Manny, what's your last name?"

"Dominguez."

"Mexican?"

"Yeah."

"By any chance, do you have a son?"

"Yeah. Two."

"Do you believe in disciplining your sons, Manny?"

"Yep."

"So Manny, what kind of discipline? Do you spank them?"

Looking at the man over his shoulder, the cab driver answered, "They're good boys, but when they talk back or don't clean their rooms, they do get disciplined."

The man in the backseat rolled his fingers into tight fists. The blood squeezed out of them, and they quivered under the pressure.

His eyelashes fluttered and his head snapped back. *This is Drago. I'll take it from here. Shut the f— up. He disciplines his sons—thinks it's OK to spank them. I think he needs to be taught a lesson.*

Drago put his right hand on top of the front seat and leaned forward; his voice now had a menacing tone. "I want you to drive to a quiet street like near a park. I need to relieve myself."

"Sure thing, boss. I'll take you to a back road near Lakeside Park." The cab driver looked in the rearview mirror to get a good look at his passenger. When his eyes met Drago's, he shuddered.

As soon as the taxi parked on the back road, Drago jumped out and pulled a knife. "Get the hell out of the car and open the trunk."

The cabbie scrambled out of the car and faced the man with the knife. "OK.OK. I don't want any trouble, here. You can have all my money."

"I said open the damn trunk!" The man pointed the knife at the driver's face.

Manny stumbled to the back of the vehicle and lifted the trunk.

Drago leaned over to check out the contents. Seeing a rope and some rags, he smiled. They'd work. He tied Manny's hands behind his back then wound the rope around his torso.

"Get in the backseat, sucker. Now!"

Manny moved toward the open door of the backseat.

Drago shoved him from behind with such force that when his forehead hit the top of the door frame, it knocked him out. Drago crammed the unconscious man into the backseat and slammed the door. After climbing into the front seat, he got on his knees and faced the backseat. *Now it's time to teach this bastard a lesson.*

He seized a fistful of Manny's hair from the back of his head and jerked him up off the seat. "It's time you learn some discipline, Manny. Wake up, dirtbag!" Drago stabbed him in the back with short, quick strokes, going in the skin deep enough to cause trickles of blood.

The sudden pain awakened the drowsy driver. He struggled and thrashed, trying to sit up, but couldn't escape the grasp of

Drago's left hand. "Hey, man!" Manny screamed. "What's with you? I didn't do anything to you!"

"Shut up. That's enough out of you." Drago took a deep breath then punched Manny three more times, knocking him out again. *That's more like it, scumbag. Stay right there and behave yourself.*

Drago laughed, turned around, fired up the engine, and drove to a picnic area closer to the lake. When he came to a dead end, he slammed on the brakes. The tires screeched and a cloud of dust and smoke caught up with the vehicle, enveloping it in a gray shroud. The smell of burning rubber replaced the fresh lake air. The taxi's engine died, but the headlights lived, shooting twin columns of light into the darkness.

The sudden stop jolted his prisoner to consciousness. A few seconds later, the cab's left rear door popped open. Manny dived out and rolled for several yards, managing to loosen the ropes enough to slide them off his wrists. He struggled to stand up then staggered in the general direction of the lake.

"You son of a bitch! You're making me mad now, Manny," Drago yelled as he leaped from the car and gave chase. He ran down his victim, tackling him to the sandy beach, a dozen yards from the water. Sitting on Manny's back, he held him down with his left hand and hit him in the back of his head with his right fist. *Did I hear his skull crack? This is getting fun. He's hurting now. It's written all over his face. What a turn-on.*

The cabbie rolled to his side and managed to throw off the attacker, then crawled toward the lake, fresh blood streaming down his back. He found a branch and took a wild upward swing that landed on Drago's forehead. The blow stunned him, and he fell to the ground.

"You shouldn't have done that, Manny. Now I'm going to have to kill you." Drago leaped on the cab driver's back, shoving his face repeatedly into the sand, breaking his nose.

Manny shrieked and pressed his fingers to his nose to stem the gushing blood. Drago continued pummeling him with an avalanche of strikes to the back of the head, ears, and face. Too weak to escape, Manny kicked his legs in a vain attempt to buck off his attacker, while the relentless blows found their mark more and more often.

Drago stretched to reach a nearby rock slightly smaller than a bowling ball. Raising it above his head, he slammed it down with a crunch. *The skull cracked that time—for sure.*

Manny's legs stopped moving, and he lay still.

Drago got up, rinsed off in the public restroom, and ran into the darkness of Lakeside Park, unaware that someone had witnessed everything.

Chapter 1

SETTING THE TRAP

"'I'm going to take down the Kingpin.' That's exactly what Carl Pickler said. I heard it with my own two ears."

"Why would Carl say that?"

Looking Thomas Whitherspoon in the eyes, Leon Rump continued. "'Cause he's after your job, that's why. Pick's an ambitious SOB who thinks you're standing in the way of his career. Ya better do something, and ya better do it quick—I'm telling ya."

Thomas Whitherspoon's heart beat faster and his breathing followed suit. His body felt hot, and the perspiration tickled him as it ran down his back. "I'll take him out," he exhaled. "I've got too much invested in this place to let a young gun take over my turf. Pickler should have more sense than to take on the Kingpin."

"Now you're talking," Rump said.

"Here's what I want you to do. Go back to your shop and compose an anonymous letter to the boss, as if you were a black employee, accusing Pickler of racism. Write it this morning. We'll kill his career if we can paint him as a racist and make it stick."

"You got it, Kingpin."

Whitherspoon poured another cup of coffee and returned to the table where they were sitting. After looking around the empty break room to ensure they were alone, he touched the chief engineer's arm and said, "Thanks, Leon. Let's keep this confidential."

Whitherspoon left the break room and walked to his cubicle. His well-defined features had improved with age, although the lines in his face had deepened. His auburn hair, colored to disguise the gray, remained thick and rich. Standing six feet three inches tall, and a stylish dresser, he reflected good health for a sixty-year-old man. But he kept his age to himself.

Arriving at his desk, Whitherspoon saw his producer, Carol Lackey, sitting in her cubicle next to his, preparing the script for the six o'clock newscast. Carol's long red hair and light complexion framed her face and brightened her smile. Single and in her late thirties, she had dedicated her life to being a TV producer. She had hoped to work as an on-air talent earlier in her career, but her weight became problematic.

Before Whitherspoon could sit down, Carol rattled off the messages she had taken for him. "Erin O'Haven, our meteorologist, wants to introduce you to her family when they visit next week from Minnesota. Jocko called to say your office remodel won't be finished for several months—the good news is that you get to stay here with me in the cubicle community—and the Briggs Lake Rotary asked you to be the featured speaker at next month's luncheon."

He nodded. "OK, put Erin's family on my calendar and tell Rotary yes. I'll speak to Jocko myself about the office. Say—waddya think of my coanchor?"

"Pickler? Good guy. Coming along. Handsome. Voice deep and pleasant—takes criticism well and everyone *loves* him."

"But can I *trust* him?" He set his coffee mug down, pushing aside some mail that had been placed on the center of his desk. "I feel I have to watch my back with him, he wants my job so bad."

"Sure you can trust him. Pick thinks you're a god. We all do. After all, you're the senior anchor. You're the Kingpin."

Thomas Whitherspoon smiled. "I wish I could be sure of that. I don't feel comfortable sharing too much with Pickler."

"I've never heard him say a bad word about you."

"Are you sure about that?" The smile on his face faded, replaced by a scowl.

That afternoon, Whitherspoon spent several hours indulging in one of his favorite pastimes: getting his hair done. Several hours of grooming included a manicure, pedicure, hairstyling with coloring. Flossie Graham, his hairstylist for the past ten years, stroked his ego along with his hair. He loved the admiration showered on him by fellow patrons, mostly women, who tried to make eye contact while Flossie worked on him and fed him the latest gossip.

Carol met him at the door when he returned to the office and followed him back to their cubicles while reading aloud her notes from a spiral notebook. "Hey, Kingpin, I got some juicy stuff for Carl Pickler's six o'clock tease. An unknown assailant attacked and killed a taxi driver named Manuel Dominguez in Lakeside Park last night."

"Where?"

"The picnic table area near the restrooms—stabbed twelve times, though that's not what killed him. Cops say that before crushing his skull, the killer tortured him with a knife. Musta been a pretty gruesome sight."

"Love it. That'll pull in viewers—good for ratings—just in time for May sweeps."

"As you like to say, boss, from your early days as a newspaper reporter, 'if it bleeds it leads.' And we got blood—lots of it. Cops are looking for a motive—nothing stolen from the taxi or the victim, so they speculate it's a hate crime."

"Suspects?"

"Not even a person of interest. I couldn't get any more details from Detective Strollo when he called Pickler, so I took down all the information and told him I'd relay it to Pickler."

Whitherspoon pulled out the chair and sat down. He swiveled to face Carol. "Let me hear what you've written so far."

"Murder in paradise at a spot for fun and pleasure. What turned a scenic picnic area, familiar to all, into a crime scene of blood and death? Tune in tonight on Briggs News 20, your source for news and information." She lowered her notepad and looked at Whitherspoon for approval.

"That's a good opening tease. You know, this murder story's too big for Pickler to handle. I should take it."

Lackey looked at Whitherspoon in disbelief. "But, boss, Pick's beat is local crime, and he's got a good relationship with Detective Strollo."

"Yeah, but Pick's got a lot to learn. This Lakeside murder's high profile, and the top guy should take it on—that's me. Give me all your notes from Strollo's call. I'll take it from here." He swallowed some coffee and turned to his desk, his body language signaling to Carol their conversation was finished.

A few minutes later, a sharp sound from Whitherspoon's cubicle startled Carol. "Did you say something?"

"Carol. What's going on here?"

His tone and volume made her involuntarily jump in her seat. "What do you mean, boss?"

"My beauty shot's askew! It's all lopsided. How could you let that happen?"

"Sorry. I guess I hadn't noticed."

"That's my favorite picture—you know that—the head shot taken when I first ascended to senior anchor. That's how I got my nickname, 'Kingpin.' Remember?" With great ceremony he straightened the framed picture temporarily mounted at the top center of his cubicle.

"I know, I know. Sorry, Tom."

"Don't let it happen again. When you get to work in the morning, always check my head shot to make sure it isn't slanted or crooked. Understand? Now, get back to work. You've got a lot to do today." Whitherspoon turned away from her and shuffled through his inbox.

"Sure. I'll remember that in the future." She slipped her hand into her purse for a tissue and dabbed her eyes.

—m—

Jocko Moore, the general manager of the TV station, opened a plain white envelope someone slid under his door and read the typed letter inside.

Dear Mr. Moore,

I'm one of your minority employees and feel you should know that Carl Pickler is a racist and has made offensive remarks that have made this a hostile work environment for blacks and Hispanics. Follow up and see for yourself. If appropriate action isn't taken, I'll sue the TV station for discrimination and creating a hostile work environment.

—Anonymous

Dropping the letter to his desk, Jocko looked out the window at the traffic below and said to himself, "Crap. Now what?"

Jocko, a heavyset man flirting with his early sixties, balding, with a ruddy-faced complexion that hinted of one too many gin and tonics, rocked his head from side to side. His current appearance gave no hint of his collegiate athletic accomplishments—some of his track records had never been surpassed. His broadcast career not only changed his physical appearance, but it also took a toll on his four marriages. As the managing partner of the LLC that owned the TV station, he enjoyed a lofty position from his early days as a sports reporter. He had a booming voice that sounded like a bass drum; it frightened secretaries and intimidated production techs.

—m—

A half hour later, Samantha Ayres, director of human resources, sat in Jocko's office reading the letter as he looked on.

When she finished and looked up, Jocko asked, "What do you make of it?"

"It appears from the language and tone, the writer's already spoken to a lawyer or had help writing it from someone who knows which words will push legal hot buttons. Look, I'm an African American and I've never noticed anything racist about Pickler, and no one has mentioned anything either. But racial discrimination and hostile work environment charges are a big deal. We have to take them seriously."

"I know," Jocko replied. "But how do you investigate Pickler among the staff without destroying his reputation with his co-workers in the process?"

Samantha didn't answer.

—m—

At the other end of the building, Pickler sat at his cubicle talking to his wife on the phone. "How ya doing, Marlene? Thought I'd check on the baby."

"Cooper's fine. In fact no change since you called a couple of hours ago."

"I can't stop thinking about him."

"Well, if you don't start thinking about your job, you're not going to have one to support this new son of yours," Marlene said.

"Good point. See you tonight. Love you."

As he ended the call, Pickler noticed a shadow move over his desk. Looking upward, he saw Whitherspoon standing over him.

"Hi, Tom."

"Hey, Pick, there's been a homicide—a jogger found a body at Lakeside Park."

"Wow!"

"Yeah. I need you to drop that feature about the girls' softball team raising money for the Wounded Warriors Project so I can have extra airtime for my special report."

Pickler's face flashed with a red shade and his expression froze. "Tom, I've been working on that feature for two weeks. I told the team they'd be on the news tonight—they're even planning a party."

"That's the news business—we gotta get a jump on breaking news ahead of the competition. Your piece can wait."

"Yeah. But isn't local crime *my* beat?" *He's stealing my story, the jealous jerk. He's green with envy over my success. Does he really think I don't know or care what he's doing to me?*

"Yes, but the powers that be want me to take this one. Sorry, Carl. It's high profile, and after all, I am the senior anchor. Thanks." Not waiting for a response, Whitherspoon turned on his heel and marched out.

Pickler felt breathless, as if he had been kicked in the stomach.

Finally collecting himself, he dialed star pitcher Hannah Strollo. "Hi, Hannah, Carl Pickler here. I'm afraid there's been a change in plans. The feature we shot on your team has been rescheduled. We had to bump the story for some breaking news. Tell everyone I'm sorry. I'll still pay for the pizzas."

—⁓—

The next day, Pickler walked into the sunny reception area of the human resources department, which smelled of jasmine and housed a fish tank. The receptionist had the day off, so the only sound he heard—the bubbling noise of the aquarium's air pump—echoed in his eardrums. He poked his head into the first office on the right. "You wanted to see me, Samantha?"

The director of human resources came out from behind her desk and extended her long, slender fingers toward one of the two vacant chairs. Those fingers reminded Pickler that in her twenties, Samantha Ayres shined as a prominent news anchor. At age forty-three, still tall, slim, and beautiful, the years had been kind to her. Not only did she still possess that on-air look, but her choice of business attire accentuated her figure and showcased her sense of style.

"Carl, I've been asked to investigate an anonymous letter that Jocko received from an employee who claims you're a racist and hostile to minorities. Is there anything to it?"

Slumping into the soft leather chair, thoughts about his newborn evaporated, replaced by bone-crushing reality. He stuttered, "A...r...re you kidding? Is this some kind of a joke? My God, that's not true. I don't have a racist bone in my body—you know that, Samantha."

Poised to write on the yellow pad resting on her crossed legs, Samantha asked, "Then, can you help me understand why someone would say that?"

Pickler spread his arms apart and shrugged. "The company picnic comes to mind. During the softball game, when I hit a single and beat the throw to first, I taunted the other team, 'Pretty fast for a white boy, ain't I?'"

"Yeah, and I remember the merciless razzing the guys gave you when you struck out the first time you came to bat. 'Whatsa matter, white boy, afraid to mess up your blond hair?'" Samantha smiled at the memory and looked down at the intersection of her black stockings and hemline. "You sure showed them."

"Yeah," Pickler said with a laugh. "We were all talking trash. Nobody took it seriously."

Samantha added, "I recall thinking at the time, 'Carl's so proud of himself to finally get a hit, we'll never hear the end of it.'"

They both laughed.

Samantha took a deep breath and refocused on the business at hand. "Anything else come to mind?"

Pickler thought for a few moments, staring at the floor before looking back at her. "Nothing," he said on a sigh. He looked out the window. His hands trembled. He gripped the sides of his chair to stop them. He knew these allegations could end his career and meant that he had a real enemy somewhere. Two streaks of sweat ran down the same side of his face as if one chased the other.

"If you think of anything, let me know. Don't discuss this with anyone."

"OK. Sure."

"Don't try to find out who sent the letter either—business as usual. OK?" she added with a steady gaze from those large, dark eyes.

"Yeah. Whatever." Getting up, he smiled at Samantha.

She nodded then looked away from him, toward the door, hiding her legendary smile and her affection for Pickler. Not even her long eye lashes waved good-bye.

Shoulders drooping, he slouched out of the office with his hands in his pockets. He felt as if his life had changed forever.

—⁓—

Hoochy's Bar and Grill, within walking distance of the TV station, didn't look like much on the outside, but the food was cheap and served fast, and it tasted homemade. It was the kind of place where waitresses called even first-time customers "honey" and "sweetie." The noise of clattering dishes, quick footsteps, and loud servers created a feeling of hurried efficiency. Thomas Whitherspoon and Carl Pickler had ordered the lunch special: sloppy joes. Pickler ordered the same dish as his mentor—an unspoken sign of respect for the older gentleman. Still shaken from that morning's meeting with Samantha Ayres, Pickler had accepted Whitherspoon's invitation to Hoochy's, glad to have a business lunch to keep his mind off the poison-pen letter.

Pickler laid his napkin on his lap. "Tom, I appreciate the invitation to lunch."

"Not a problem. Say, Pick, I'm a little short of cash. Would you mind picking up the tab?"

"Sure. Can we talk confidentially?" Pickler looked around the restaurant while he waited for an answer.

The question jolted Whitherspoon's attention from admiring his reflection in a nearby mirror. He turned to face Pickler. "Sure. What's on your mind?" Reaching for his water glass, he took a long gulp, which made such a loud sound they both smiled.

In the next instant, a ruckus at the front door diverted their attention. A man yelled like a squawking chicken, "Shut up! Don't say anything!" as two men dragged him outside.

The confused scene distracted them long enough for Pickler to recall the admonition from Samantha not to discuss their meeting with anyone. He changed course. "I wanted to thank you for supporting me and sharing your wisdom on how to be a successful news anchor."

"Forget it, kid. Say, how's your little son doing?"

"He's adorable. Cooper acts like me and looks like his mother." Pickler inhaled, which made his chest stick out.

"Good thing he looks like Marlene," Whitherspoon said with a smile.

Pickler smiled and nodded. "We'd like you to be his godfather, Tom. Would you consider it?"

"Yeah, no problem. Have Carol Lackey put it on my calendar." Whitherspoon slurped his water and this time made a sucking sound. He looked away from Pickler, glancing at his reflection in the mirror and then toward the kitchen. "When's that food gonna get here?"

—๛—

Back at Samantha Ayres's office, Leon Rump shifted in his chair. He had requested the meeting. "Samantha, before I go on, promise you'll keep this between us. I gotta work with these guys."

Not about to promise Rump anything, she took a deep breath to brace herself for the news he was about to share. Nobody ever asked to meet with her to share happy news. Her fingers tensed on the pen, ready to write on her yellow pad. "Please continue."

Rump noticed her manicured fingernails. To him they looked like tabs of polished porcelain. His eyes remained fixed on her fingers as he spoke. "I heard Pick use the N-word. It shocked me. I walked past his cubicle and heard him say it to describe an alleged rapist, to someone on the phone. He must have been preparing a story for the news." He looked back up at Samantha.

"What exactly did he say, Leon?"

Rump fidgeted with his short gray ponytail, adjusted his baseball cap, and pulled his t-shirt down over his beer belly. "Pick said, 'That damned n—.' I won't even say the word. My apologies to you, Ms. Ayres. I got outta there fast—didn't say anything to him."

"Anyone else around at the time?" Out of the corner of her eye, Samantha noticed he had begun tapping his foot on the floor, but she continued to look at his unshaven face, waiting for an answer.

"Yes, there were people around, but I forgot who. Sorry."

"What else, Leon?"

"The intern—last summer before she left for school, Fannie said Pick told her he hated blacks and Hispanics and would make sure none ever got into the anchor's chair."

"Are you sure? Doesn't sound like Pick." Samantha jotted notes on the yellow pad. Her jaw tightened. "Why didn't Fannie report it to me?"

"Fannie thought getting involved in a controversy might damage her future in broadcasting—you know, if like, she made a stink about it and got known as a whistle-blower." Rump rubbed his hands together.

Samantha's eyebrows arched. After a few seconds of silence, she said, "Why'd you decide to tell me all this today?" She stared at him.

"What do ya mean?" He fidgeted.

"This all happened some time ago. Why are you telling me now?"

"I dunno. I been busy, I guess. Thought you should know. That's all."

She flashed a brief smile. "Thanks, Leon." She rose to shake his hand and felt it wet with sweat. He turned and bolted down the hall.

Samantha walked to the window and looked out at nothing in particular. She folded her arms, her posture erect, and her thoughts a million miles away. The phone rang. Returning to her desk and standing behind it, she answered.

"Well, what did you come up with?" Jocko demanded.

"Rump heard Pick use the N-word," Samantha replied.

"Anyone else hear Pick say it?"

"No. But Leon said the summer intern, Fannie, heard Pick say something to the effect that he would make sure no blacks or Hispanics would ever make it to the anchor chair. She didn't want to be known as a whistle-blower. That's why she didn't say anything to me. I'll call her to verify his story."

Jocko exhaled slowly, puffing out both cheeks. "Doesn't sound like Pick."

"I thought the same thing. Leon seemed pretty sure of what he heard."

Jocko cleared his throat. "I'm afraid it's time to look for another coanchor in case we have to make a change. It will take a long time to find a good fit. Keep me posted. Thanks."

Samantha put the receiver down and looked out the window. Most days she loved her job—not today. She felt a stomach cramp followed by a dizzy feeling. Sinking into her desk chair, she emptied her lungs with a groan.

—ᗯ—

After eating lunch with Pickler, Whitherspoon drove to the police station to see Detective Louis Strollo, the man in charge of the Lakeside Park homicide investigation. Whitherspoon figured Strollo would be the best source for a nightly series on the slaying. After being admitted to Strollo's office, Whitherspoon spoke first. "I know you usually work with Carl Pickler, but the powers that be have asked me to take over the story. This is huge, and our viewers prefer getting their important news from me."

The homicide detective sat on the edge of his desk, tie loosened and sleeves rolled up. The son of Italian immigrants, and a twenty-year veteran of the force, Strollo earned the respect of all who knew him. Though in his midforties, he projected a vitality and strength, his hair still naturally pitch-black, complemented by a well-trimmed mustache.

"No offense, but I'm sorry to hear the station pulled him off the story. Pick's a good guy. Knows his stuff, a real pro." Strollo looked Whitherspoon in the eye. "Here's the situation: we have no murder weapon, no suspects and no witnesses—just a body."

"I can put your Crime Solvers Hotline number on every news package. I'm sure you'll get viewer responses—my fans will be all over this," Whitherspoon said.

Strollo nodded. "Good. Hopefully someone will come forward who has seen or heard something unusual."

"I plan to do a series on the progress of your investigation," Whitherspoon said.

Strollo shook his head. "Right now we have no witnesses, so I don't think we have enough information to give you a series of news shows."

"I'll decide what's newsworthy." Whitherspoon fixed his eyes on Strollo. "Just give me direct access to you and regular updates. That's all I ask."

"With all due respect, Mr. Whitherspoon, I'm in charge of this investigation, not you. This will not turn into a media circus, and I'm not your puppet. It's not about you, your evening news, or your TV station. This is about solving a homicide." Strollo slid off the desktop, to a standing position, hands at his sides, and glared at Whitherspoon.

"Hey, man, cool your jets," Whitherspoon said, holding up both palms as if to push him away.

Strollo's expression was as firm as his tone. "Back off. There's a protocol I follow to maintain the legality and integrity of the investigation."

"You're my go-to guy. That's all I'm saying," Whitherspoon said.

Strollo moved behind his desk and sat down in the chair. "I'll give you some facts as we go along. Be real careful how you use them. I have to conceal certain things so the killer doesn't know how much I know."

"Then we understand each other." Whitherspoon took out his minirecorder. "Now, tell me what you can about the wounds found on the body." Whitherspoon pushed Record and smiled.

—m—

While Whitherspoon and Strollo were meeting, Rump, in his workshop, placed a call to the college student who had interned at the station during her summer vacation.

"Hey. Is this Fannie Larsen? Leon Rump here from Briggs News 20. How's school going? Great. Remember when you told me you'd do anything to get into broadcasting? Well, I have something I want you to do for me."

—⚏—

The next morning Whitherspoon asked Jocko if they could meet to discuss some important station issues. As they settled in their chairs in Jocko's office, he asked, "What's up, Kingpin?"

"Jocko, when's my office going to be done? You promised it would be done by now, and it's not done. I'm not happy. It isn't right for the senior anchor to be sitting in a bullpen of cubicles with a bunch of producers and their staffs."

"The building inspector has been slow in giving us the necessary building permits. That said, we should be back on track soon and complete the last stage of the remodel in a few months." Jocko shrugged.

"And one thing I want to make sure: is mine still going to be the biggest office?"

Jocko grinned. "Yes, and as you requested, we're installing a full-length mirror and your own private restroom."

"Excellent." Whitherspoon beamed. "What about the makeup room?"

"Yeah, that too." Jocko's smile evaporated. "You'll have a private makeup room as you requested."

"Any word from the board members about my clothing allowance?"

Jocko frowned. "Sorry. They don't think paying for your suits is necessary since Briggs Lake is more casual than most cities and not a major market."

"They don't get it, do they?" Whitherspoon grimaced.

"Money's tight with the economy the way it is."

Whitherspoon furrowed his brow. "I know Briggs Lake is more laid-back, but consider this: I'm the number one guy in this market, and I need to dress like it."

"Bring up the clothing allowance when you renegotiate your contract next February."

"I'm the high-end real estate around here, Jocko. You know that."

"You're the Kingpin, that's for sure," Jocko replied, folding his arms and scanning his office to avoid eye contact with Whitherspoon.

Whitherspoon got up and paced back and forth. "I hope my age doesn't have anything to do with those suits blowing me off. I'll slap them with an age-discrimination legal motion faster than—"

"Relax. I don't think you have anything to worry about there." After saying this, Jocko got up and put his hand on Whitherspoon's shoulder. "Hell, I'm older than you are. If they based decisions on age, they'd have gotten rid of my ass by now."

"It's not the same thing, Jocko. You're a GM and managing partner. You've got job security. I'm an on-air talent. They want those young faces in people's living rooms. My only protection is my contract."

Jocko lumbered to the desk and grabbed his coffee mug. He sipped from it, made a face, and set the mug back on his desk. "You worry way too much about your age."

Whitherspoon took a deep breath, nodded, and settled back into his chair. He pushed his hand along the seam of his suit pants to straighten a small wrinkle. Sitting up straighter, he looked back at Jocko and continued. "I just hope they appreciate what they have—that's all I'm saying. Sometimes I don't feel the love."

"News is a business, not a lovefest. The board thinks you're doing a great job and so do I. Stop stressing out over it," Jocko said.

"Oh yeah? You know as well as I do, the company takes youth over experience every time. I've put a lot of myself into this news show, and I'm an iconic figure in Briggs Lake. You'd lose viewers if you dumped me for a younger anchor. That's a fact, Jocko." Whitherspoon got up from his chair and brushed some lint off his lapel. He looked at himself in the mirror, turning his head to the left and then to the right, preening like a parrot. The corners of his mouth turned up, and a sparkle flashed in his eyes as he sat back down.

Jocko touched his fists together. "You better be careful talking money when you negotiate your next contract. You don't want to price yourself out of the market, big guy. If you do, those younger—and cheaper—anchors are gonna start looking pretty good to them."

"I'm their meal ticket, and they know it," Whitherspoon declared.

"Cool it. Don't push management too far. I'm saying this for your own good," Jocko said.

"Here's an example of what I'm talking about. Strollo's feeding me stuff he's not giving to anyone else on the Lakeside murder—exclusives, baby. My ratings will go through the roof. That'll mean big bucks for the station in advertising revenue, and it'll make you and the board look like geniuses."

"Hey, Tom, I thought we agreed Pick would cover local crime stories." Jocko's tone of voice revealed an agitation he took no pains to disguise.

Whitherspoon scowled and wrapped his fingers around the armrests of his chair. "The kid and I both felt that it's so high profile I should get it. He's not as confident as I am, and his reporting needs more of an edge. But I'm working with him on those things."

"I think you're *both* doing a great job, and Pick's not a kid. I like the whole look and feel of our news. Pick's getting quite a fan following and good reviews—I get a lot of nice letters and e-mails about his work."

"But...are you getting as many compliments on Pick as you're getting on me?" Whitherspoon leaned forward with his elbows on the arms of the chair. "Huh?"

Jocko bit into his lower lip. "No." After saying that, he turned his back on Whitherspoon and began organizing papers and straightening file folders.

"That's what I thought." Relieved, Whitherspoon got up, looking triumphant. "One more thing. Did Carol tell you about my beauty shot?"

"You mean your headshot?"

"Yeah. I want my beauty shot hung in a prominent place in my new office where everyone will see it."

"OK."

"Keep in mind, it should never be crooked. People should check it all the time to make sure it's straight."

"Sure."

"Good. I'm glad we understand each other. See ya." Whitherspoon pranced out of the office.

Jocko shrugged without looking up.

—⁓—

Later in the day, Whitherspoon and Rump sat at a corner table in Hoochy's so Whitherspoon could see himself in the mirror while they ate lunch. "So, what happened with that intern Fannie?" Whitherspoon asked.

"I told Fannie to expect a call from Samantha and all she has to say is something about hearing Pick talk about how he hated blacks and Hispanics and would make sure none would ever get on air." After saying this, Rump took a napkin and wiped the ketchup from his mouth with a broad swiping motion, back and forth like a harmonica player. His technique left a couple of red smears on his face.

Whitherspoon looked away from Rump and toward the mirror to check his hair. He liked the way his hair looked today. He ran his right hand over a few rebellious strands to put them back in place. *Perfect*, he thought. "What did you promise her in exchange for helping us?"

"A recommendation from you, help with her demo when she graduates, and some cash."

"Cash? How much?"

"Never mind. It's not much. I want to help the girl out. I'll cover it."

A smile swept across Whitherspoon's face. "I gotta thank you, Leon, for tipping me off to Pickler's scheme." He rested both hands palms down on the table. *Carol said she never heard the guy say a bad word about me. If she's right, I could end up destroying the career of one of my biggest supporters.*

To escape the troubling thought, Whitherspoon caught his reflection in the mirror again. *Damn, my hair's looking so good today. No wonder everyone has their eye on me.*

"Forget it, Kingpin," Rump said. "I've been glad to help you."

"Look, I appreciate your help and all, but why are you doing all this for me?" Whitherspoon flexed his jaw muscles.

"You're the star here, and I wanna make sure nothing changes that." Rump patted his gut with both hands. "Damn, that was a good burger."

Whitherspoon moved closer to the table and whispered, "OK, look, I want you to leave a voice message for Flip Connors that investigative reporter for the *Canyon Times*—an anonymous tip that there's an internal investigation of racism at Briggs News 20, involving on-air talent. Get my drift?" Whitherspoon raised his eyebrows and smirked, then chuckled with delight, his head bobbing up and down. He stopped himself in mid-guffaw to smooth an errant strand of hair back in place.

Rump laughed until he started coughing at Whitherspoon's uncharacteristic display of emotion. He nodded. "Yeah, when that bulldog calls Jocko for confirmation, he'll crap his pants," he chortled. "You're a frickin' genius, Kingpin...a frickin' genius."

Whitherspoon sat a little taller, cocked his face, and checked his likeness in the mirror one more time. He smiled with admiration and liked what he saw. *I'll say this for Rump—he gets me.*

Chapter 2

WITNESS TO MURDER

"You're outta there!" The umpire shot his hand to the right, indicating a strike. The batter had struck out, and the large crowd cheered. The Briggs Lake Hellcats were battling the Palmer Pearls, their archrivals, in a high school softball game. Carl and Marlene Pickler were seated on the aluminum bleachers behind home plate with their baby son, Cooper, who had fallen asleep in his daddy's arms despite the commotion.

When the Hellcats ran from the infield toward their bench after the inning, Pickler yelled at the pitcher, "Nice work, Hannah!"

Hannah Strollo sat down on the bench, then turned to look at Pickler and beamed.

Pickler, a first-team All-American baseball pitcher for Arizona State, met Marlene at college. He considered a pro career, but journalism was his passion. She captained the Sun Devils women's softball team and played catcher. Although both graduated with honors, their athletic accomplishments overshadowed their academic work. Carl was named the most valuable player on his team in his senior year, and Marlene had been voted into the school's athletic hall of fame.

"Carl, you'd make an inspirational softball coach," Marlene said with a smile. "You sure know the game and how to motivate players. They respond to you."

"Well, thank you, Miss Marlene, but I'd rather watch and support the team. Coaching would take too much time away from you and little Cooper." He reached over with his right arm and gave her a squeeze, careful to balance the baby he cradled in his left.

Marlene leaned on his shoulder and sighed. "No argument here. There's nothing that compares with spending time with you." She smiled again.

Pickler loved the way his wife, after making any powerful statement, would emphasize it with a wide smile, an endearing characteristic and one he had tried to emulate, without much success.

"You keep getting hotter every day. What's your secret?" Pickler gushed.

"Stop it," she said.

"Your smokin'-good looks on the outside are only surpassed by your sizzling beauty on the inside."

"You're so full of it."

"Your hair may look like sunshine, but your heart is twenty-four-karat gold."

"I knew you majored in Journalism, but it looks like you got a minor in BS." Marlene blushed, got up to adjust her side of the padded blanket, and then looked around to see if anyone had heard their conversation. Satisfied that fans were occupied with the action on the field, she sat back down.

"Carl, why don't you let people see your athleticism? You always pretend to be clumsy, awkward, and weak at events like company picnics. I don't get it."

"I don't want to come across like a showboat. Let others shine."

"If you got it, flaunt it, baby!" Marlene fired right back and punctuated the end of the sentence with that killer smile.

"If you got it, you don't *need* to flaunt it," he answered, then remembered to add the smile at the end. Each tried to stare the other down.

Detective Strollo interrupted their stare-down when he shouted above the din of the crowd, "So how're the Picklers?"

"Awesome, Louie. You missed seeing Hannah strike out the last batter. It was a fastball, high and tight." Pickler began demonstrating, then stopped after glancing at Cooper and realizing he held a baby in his arm. "It's a pitcher's duel, a close game."

"Just my luck. Now that I'm here, they'll probably take her out of the game."

"No way—not the way your daughter's throwing heat," Marlene confirmed.

"Say, Carl, I hate to talk shop, but why is Whitherspoon covering the Lakeside killing for your station? Why not you? What gives?" Strollo held his hands out as though waiting to receive something.

"This is different. High profile, Louie. The powers that be think Mr. Whitherspoon should take it. He *is* the senior anchor after all." Pickler shrugged and looked back at the game.

"OK, see you guys later." Strollo moved away for a closer look at the action on the playing field.

Marlene turned to her husband. "Carl, you didn't tell me Whitherspoon took over coverage of the Lakeside murder. When did that happen?" This time there was no smile when she finished speaking.

"A while ago." Pickler remained focused on the infield.

"Why didn't you *say* something?" Marlene demanded.

"Nothing to say."

"Who are these 'powers that be?' The voices in Kingpin's head?"

"Jocko, I assume. He's the boss. Say, not to change the subject, but Mr. Whitherspoon agreed to be Cooper's godfather. Isn't that great?" Pickler's face broke into a big grin as he looked over at Marlene.

"Oh, that's great...just great." Marlene looked away.

—◦◦◦—

The umpire yelled, "Game over!" Hannah Strollo's ponytail flopped up and down in the center of a pinwheel of softball caps, gloves, and uniforms. The high-pitched voices shrieking and cheering became the soundtrack of the scene. The Briggs Lake Hellcats had defeated the Palmer Pearls 2–0. Hannah Strollo's dominating pitching kept opposing batters from getting even a single hit. She struck out twelve of the twenty-four batters she faced with speed and pinpoint accuracy. Her teammates huddled around, patting her back, giving her high fives and fist bumps in a joyful circle of celebration.

No one in the congratulatory chaos noticed Hannah's father taking it all in, standing alone, in a wrinkled white shirt and a loosened tie. *If only her mother could have lived to see this. She would have been so proud to see her daughter in this moment of victory, so happy and so loved by others.* He absorbed the spectacle the way a front-row theater patron soaks up the sights and sounds of a favorite play.

The curtain came down too soon on Strollo's wife, who had died of cancer. He missed his wife and thought about her every day. Throughout the day, he still found himself thinking *Cancer sucks.* He coped with his loss by pouring himself into his work. Hannah became the center of his universe and main reason for living. Colleagues respected Strollo, and criminals feared him. His relentless work ethic and attention to detail propelled him to the position of chief homicide detective. The upward trajectory of his career was fueled by his many accomplishments, but his personal life was on empty and the warning light was on.

When the gaggle of girls thinned out, Strollo walked up to his daughter and embraced her. "I'm so proud of you." He choked up so he rested his chin on her shoulder.

"Thanks, Dad. Say, I know we talked about going out to dinner, but the team's going to a restaurant to celebrate together. Do you mind if I cancel out on our hot date? We can have dinner anytime."

"Ah...no problem. I have some work to do anyway. See you later at home. Don't stay out too late, now." He squeezed her again and kissed her cheek. Hannah's tumultuous teammates recaptured her attention, and she joined them in chanting, "Briggs Lake! Briggs Lake! Briggs Lake!" Caught up in the excitement, she didn't notice her dad walking away, his shoulders drooping like old curtains.

—m—

Since the softball fields were adjacent to Lakeside Park, Strollo thought this a good opportunity to take another look at the crime scene that had shaken the residents of Briggs Lake. He hoped that this, his seventh visit, would shed some light on the death of an innocent man. He followed up on every lead from the anonymous tip line, but each was a bridge to nowhere. He needed a break in the case, and he needed one soon.

While trying to visualize the sequence of events leading to the savage beating of an innocent man, Strollo heard a voice behind him.

"You're investigating the killing, ain't ya?"

Strollo swiveled around and put his hand near his service revolver. Standing in front of him, an unshaven old man wearing ragged shorts, worn sandals, and a stained t-shirt trained his clear blue eyes on the detective.

Strollo exhaled. "How'd you know?"

"Don't matter. I saw the whole thing. Lately I bin sleepin' under that bush by the restrooms."

"Anything you can tell me will be helpful." Strollo's face relaxed, revealing a slight smile under his mustache.

"I woke up when I heard brakes screeching and saw a man dive out the back door. The guy rolled out after the car stopped and the dust caught up with it."

"What kinda car?" Strollo pulled out a notepad and took notes.

"I dunno. A taxi...a shuttle...something like that."

"What happened next?"

"I smelt burning rubber. The engine quit but the headlights stayed on. I saw him get up."

"Who?"

"The guy from the backseat who dived out. Pardon me, you wouldn't happen to have a smoke on you by any chance?"

"No. Sorry. What'd the guy look like?"

"Thin. Looked like a Mexican."

"How could you tell?" Strollo asked.

"Light from the headlights and a full moon."

"What'd he do?"

"He laid there for a few seconds, then got up and ran for the lake."

"Show me where." Strollo stopped writing and looked at the man.

"Right over there." The man stepped over the foot-high retaining wall and pointed to an area near the lake.

Strollo walked to the spot and knelt down, staring at the sand for a few seconds. Then, looking back up at the man, he asked, "What about the driver?"

"He got out and chased him."

"What'd he look like?"

"A white guy, 'bout the same size, I'd say." He scratched the back of his head as though the gesture would stimulate his memory.

"Did he carry a knife or a gun or any kind of weapon?" Strollo asked.

"Don't think so. Didn't see any. The guy ran him down and tackled him to the ground. He never made it to the lake."

"Did the victim fight back?"

"Not at first. The attacker sat on the other guy's back and held him down with his left hand and with his right hand punched him on the back a the head over and over."

"Could you hear what they were saying? Were they arguing about something?" Strollo asked.

"Nope...thought the Mexican guy stopped breathing, 'cause he laid there so still. Then he got up and crawled toward the lake... could see blood streaming down his back."

"Anyone else around?"

"Can't say for sure. Next thing that happened, the Mexican found a stick on the ground and from his knees turned and whacked the guy right in the head—knocked him down."

"Where?"

"Over there." The man pointed toward another area and walked over to it. "Pretty quick after that, he got back up, yelled something, and jumped on the Mexican's back. He pounded him—face-first—into the sand, again and again." The man demonstrated using both hands.

Strollo ran his finger across his mustache. "What happened next?"

"Musta broke the Mexican's nose—all that bashing in the sand. Blood gushed everywhere."

"Did he keep fighting back?"

"No. I heard the man crying. He kicked his legs, trying to get the guy off him. The white guy musta found a big rock nearby, 'cause he raised some object high up in the air with both hands and smashed it down on the Mexican's head. Made a crunching sound. No crying after that—and the legs stopped moving, too."

"How long would you say this took?"

"A few minutes."

"Then what happened?"

"The white guy got up, walked to the restroom, washed all the blood off—stumbled right past me, but didn't see me 'cause a the bush—put something in the trash can, and ran away."

"What'd he put in the trash?"

"Couldn't see."

"Come on, you were close by—full moon and the restroom has lights. What'd he put in the trash? You must have seen something."

"Your detectives already went through the trash can, and you know what he put in there—paper towels smeared with blood. Are you testing me?"

Strollo ignored the question. "Where'd the guy run to?"

"I dunno. Just took off."

"Didn't you try to help the guy on the ground?"

"Nah...he was dead already, nothing I could do. Found a couple in a parked car, going at it, and asked them to call the cops. I did what I could do."

"So, you must be the homeless guy they told us about." Strollo stepped closer to the man to get a better look at him.

"Yep."

"What's your name?"

"They call me Eli."

"Mr. Eli, I'll need to take you to the police station so you can make a sworn statement." Strollo called the office to make the necessary arrangements. When he ended the call and turned around, Eli was gone.

Chapter 3

GAME CHANGER

"Hey, man, d'ya have some spare change? I need something to eat."

Whitherspoon had driven to work as giddy as a frat boy at a beer pong tournament. He had orchestrated a fatal blow to Pickler's career, his office remodel would soon be completed, and his hair looked spectacular today. Seeing this old and dirty man on the bench begging for money jolted him from elation to irritation.

"Hey, loser, you're a real buzzkill. Get a job." Whitherspoon's voice blared like a megaphone.

The man glared at him with bright, glowing eyes. "You shouldn't speak to people that way."

"Maybe you shouldn't be asking people for handouts. Outta my way before I call the cops." Whitherspoon waved his arm at the vagrant and scaled the steps to the Briggs News 20 studio.

When Carol Lackey observed her boss striding in her direction, she could tell something had upset him. She decided to cheer him up.

"So, we're keeping bankers' hours now, boss?" she teased, a devilish smile on her face.

"Excuse me, Producer Lackey. Sorry to keep you waiting. Didn't realize you'd be arriving early from *WeightWatchers*. How'd the weigh-in go?" He smiled.

"You should have been a comedian," Carol said. "You're hilarious, Kingpin."

"That's 'Mr. Kingpin' to you."

"Whatsa matter, is your big, bruised ego in need of stroking again?"

"The only thing needing stroking is the script you're supposed to write," he grumbled.

"Is your sense of humor in the witness protection program?"

Whitherspoon laughed in spite of himself. "You're the one good at standup comedy. Good thing too—you'll need some way to make a living after I fire you. If you must know, I've been shopping for new suits, since this company's too damn cheap to buy them for me. I'm the number one news guy in this city, and I gotta look the part."

"Well, Mr. Top-News-Guy, Detective Strollo called." Lackey handed him a phone message. "Says it's important."

"That's good. I'm expecting updates. He's supposed to share information as he develops his investigation so I can keep my fans informed of his progress." Whitherspoon sat down at his cubicle and dialed Strollo.

Strollo answered on the first ring. "Detective Strollo speaking."

"Whitherspoon here. You left a message?"

"Yeah. I need your help with something. I interviewed a witness to the Lakeside murder yesterday, but before I could get him to the police station to sign his statement, he took off. Would you ask your viewers if anyone witnessed the murder, or anything unusual at Lakeside Park, to contact the police department?"

"I'll mention it tonight on the newscast," Whitherspoon said.

"Great. Have them call the Crime Solvers Hotline so I can follow up on their leads."

"Will do. Keep me updated." Whitherspoon hung up and turned to Lackey. "Excellent. I guess I bought my new suits just in time."

—∞—

That evening, Briggs News 20 went on the air. "Quiet on the set. Three...two...one...rolling!" The floor director nodded to Whitherspoon.

"Good evening, I am Thomas Whitherspoon, and he's Carl Pickler. Briggs News 20 starts now."

The wide shot of the two switched to a close-up of Whitherspoon, who looked straight into the camera.

"Two weeks ago Manuel Dominguez, a local cab driver, was beaten to death at Lakeside Park. The killer is a white male with a medium build. It looks as if nothing was stolen from the victim or taxi, so investigators must speculate on the motive. A man named Eli claimed to witness the slaying but has since been out of the public eye. He remains a person of interest. If you saw anything out of place at the park, or if you know the whereabouts of Eli, call the Crime Solvers Hotline and leave an anonymous tip. The number is displayed right now at the bottom of your TV screen."

Whitherspoon and Pickler took turns reading their scripts from the teleprompter. They reported on the many activities taking place in the area: special events, youth baseball scores, and the fishing report.

Erin O' Haven, "The Weather Maven," as she liked to be called, delivered one of her humorous monologues on the repetitious forecasts of desert weather. "Today's forecast in Briggs Lake is for more sun and heat...like yesterday and the day before, and the day before that. And you know what? I'll go out on a limb here. It's going to be sunny and hot next week as well." She laughed. "This is Erin O'Haven, your weather maven. Back to you, Tom."

The time had arrived for Ronnie Gaboni to give the sports report. He made no claim to any athletic background himself, and one look at his rotund frame would dispel any thought to the contrary. The only sport one could imagine him competing in would be a hot dog-eating contest. Eating seemed to energize his reporting the way turning a key starts a car. Rumors suggested Gaboni was a closeted pool shark, though he never talked about it. One could imagine him playing in pool tournaments, especially if it involved food.

As the show came to an end, the director switched to the wide shot, cut the volume on the mics, and rolled music and credits. "Clear!"

"Good job, Tom. I liked the way you described the sequence of facts in the homicide investigation," Pickler said to Whitherspoon.

Whitherspoon looked over at Pickler as he handed his earpiece and battery pack to the audio tech. "Thanks."

Erin approached Whitherspoon. "I wanted to say thanks for agreeing to meet my parents. They're big fans. Carol has it all set up. You're such a cool dude."

"No problem." With a slight wave, Whitherspoon scooted out the door and made a beeline for the engineering shop to see Leon Rump.

When Rump saw Whitherspoon at his doorway, he dropped some of the cables he had been untangling. "Kingpin, don't believe that backstabbing Pickler. I heard what he said to you after the show from my studio monitor. I don't like the way he kisses your ass to your face and stabs you when your back is turned. He told me this morning you were a dinosaur. You gotta watch your back with Pickler around."

"I guess I do, Leon. You wanted to see me?"

"Yeah, I'm going to take a little trip to visit Fannie and give her the money. She goes to Arizona State at the Tempe campus. She did good by backing up my story with Samantha."

"Tempe's a long drive. Why not mail it?"

"Some things are better done in person." Rump smiled and rubbed his hands together.

"Say, has Samantha gotten back with any follow-up on your meeting where you told her about Pickler using the N-word and Fannie's comment?"

"Nothing. Haven't heard a thing. I'm sure she's doing something with it. Thanks for helping me write that anonymous letter. I ain't so good at writing."

"Glad to help people who are helping me." Whitherspoon pointed at Rump. "You're the man. See you later."

"No. You're the man. You're the Kingpin." Rump replied.

Whitherspoon smiled and strutted out of the room.

—⁓—

The next night Rump enjoyed dinner and drinks with Fannie Larsen at a restaurant near Arizona State's campus. The food was average and the service poor. He had chosen the spot because it offered cheap liquor. Tempe residents, well aware of its low standards, avoided the bistro, as evidenced by the few customers in attendance for a Saturday night.

"Thanks, Mr. Rump. You didn't have to drive all the way here to pay me," Fannie said after dinner. Five feet tall, slightly overweight for her size, her blond hair and cream-colored skin gave her face an angelic appearance. The few diners who dared eat at the joint couldn't take their eyes off her. Fannie knew her looks attracted stares, and she enjoyed the attention.

"It's the least I can do. Don't tell anyone. It's our little secret," Rump said.

"I'm good at keeping secrets, Mr. Rump. Actually, I'm good at a lot of things." She tilted her head forward and smiled, revealing two dimples and ample cleavage.

"Good girl, Fannie. You don't have to call me Mr. Rump. Leon's fine." Rump put his hand on her knee under the table and looked into her blue eyes. "You want another drink?"

"Sure, Leon. I'm a little dizzy. Can you get me something a little weaker this time?" Her face flushed and droplets of perspiration emerged on her forehead.

"Get used to it. When you graduate, business is done over dinner and drinks. You gotta learn how to handle yourself." He waved to the server. "Another round here! A beer for me and a strawberry daiquiri for the lady."

"I'm willing to do anything at all to get to the top of this business. You need to know that. You could say I'm real ambitious." She placed her hand on top of his under the table.

"I'm getting that feeling." Rump smiled.

When the server arrived, he removed his hand from her knee, plucking the bottle from the table and hoisting it to his lips in one swift movement.

Fannie took a swig of her daiquiri and burped. "Excuse me. Say, when're you gonna help me make my audiss...shun tape?"

"We'll work on the audition reel in a month or so when things quiet down at the station. No worries. I gotcha covered, babe." After a second drink of beer, he wiped his mouth with the back of his hand.

Witnessing his imbibing inspired Fannie to follow suit. She didn't like the feeling she got when she sipped her daiquiri, yet she felt she should try to keep up with Rump. "I th-th-hink I need to get back to my dorm. I don't feel so good."

"Not a problem." He chugged the remainder of his bottle, paid the tab, and led her to his Chevy Suburban. He unlocked it from the driver's side and motioned for her to get in. Fannie opened the passenger door and plunked herself down on the front seat. She leaned her head against the window and fell asleep.

She awoke when the car stopped on an isolated desert road. Still groggy, she tried to sit up, only to be shoved down. Rump popped open the snap on her waist then yanked her shorts and panties past her knees, tugging at them until they cleared her ankles. He climbed on top of her.

"Please don't, Leon—"

He nuzzled her neck and cheek. "Don't you remember you said you'd do anything for your career? Well, I'm gonna help your career, and you're gonna give me some things too. That's the way it works in the real world."

"Stop it. I don't feel good," she pleaded.

"When I'm done with you, you're going to feel great." Rump forced his tongue into her mouth. She moved her head from side to side to disengage the oral assault, feeling her face getting scratched by his whiskers.

She pushed up with her hands until they had no more strength, then her arms collapsed to her sides. Fannie closed her eyes and waited for it to be over.

—m—

"She confirmed Pick made disparaging remarks about African Americans and says she heard him say he'd make sure no blacks ever made it to the anchor's chair." Samantha paused to see what effect Fannie's words were having on Jocko Moore.

"Well, OK...if that's what she heard...But it still doesn't sound like Pick," Jocko said.

"I asked Fannie why she didn't report it at the time, and she said she thought being a whistle-blower would hurt her career."

"Not if she's telling the truth."

"That's what I told her. She still won't go public. Her future career means everything, and I got the impression she'll do anything for it," Samantha said.

"Now what?" Jocko paced back and forth, his hands behind his back.

"We could meet with all the black employees at the same time and ask them about Pick."

"Yeah, but if he's innocent, we'll ruin his reputation."

"OK, then we wouldn't have to mention his name. We could discuss the anonymous letter and ask the writer to privately give us specifics." Samantha's cell phone rang, and she scooped it up from her chair's armrest.

"Yes, this is Samantha Ayres....Where did you hear that?" Her eyes darted toward Jocko, who looked wide-eyed back at her. "We don't comment on personnel matters: company policy. OK. Thanks for the advance notice. Good-bye."

"Who was that?" Jocko asked.

"A newspaper reporter received an anonymous tip about my investigation. They're doing a big article and wanted us to tell our side of the story for balance."

"What's his name and who does he work for?"

"Flip Connors from the *Canyon Times*," she said.

"Holy crap! He's their investigative reporter. He's a shark and smells blood in the water." Jocko massaged his bald head as though something had just struck it.

"I wonder who tipped him off." Samantha said and exhaled heavily. "This is a game changer."

Jocko nodded. "I gotta get with the board right away and let them know what's going down. Send me an e-mail summarizing your investigation and make a recommendation, and I'll forward it to the board with my comments. We'll see what they wanna do."

"We have two days before they go with the story." Samantha walked out of Jocko's office, leaving him staring out the window with his hands behind his back.

—⁂—

Later that day, Samantha's assistant ushered Strollo into her office.

"Detective Strollo, I'm Samantha Ayres. Nice to meet you." She extended her hand. They held their grip a little longer than necessary for the normal business handshake. "Please sit down."

"Thank you for meeting with me on such short notice." His gaze journeyed from her wide, almond-shaped brown eyes to her broad shoulders before traveling down her charcoal gray business suit, which didn't hide her well-proportioned figure. He admired the shape of her long, slender fingers and noted that she wasn't wearing a wedding ring.

"What can I do for you?" Samantha studied her visitor with great interest. She felt her heart accelerating and as if a magnetic force was drawing her to him.

"My investigation into the Lakeside homicide has led me to believe there might be a connection to Briggs News 20. I would like to work closely with you due to the sensitive nature of the matter. This may involve employees and high profile news personnel. Your cooperation will be very helpful to my work."

"I must tell you, sir—when we have open positions, I do not fill them with assassins."

"Oh, I'm sure. I didn't mean to say one of your employees killed someone—only that collected forensic evidence from the crime scene indicates a possible link to your TV station."

"Sorry. I didn't mean to sound...Please go on." Samantha adjusted her sitting position and crossed her legs.

Strollo looked down at her legs, lingering on their attractive shape, sculpted to perfection, hiding under black stockings and a form-fitting business skirt.

"We'd like to conduct DNA tests on some of your employees and compare results with DNA found at the scene. We can test their DNA without their knowledge, but the prosecutor's office is deciding whether or not the evidence would be admissible in court. Do you have a company policy regarding this?"

"Never has come up, Detective. I would think we could test their DNA only with their prior knowledge and permission. If served a court order, we wouldn't have any choice in the matter. I'll check with Corporate and get their guidance." She jotted a note on her yellow pad. "I'll get back to you if you can give me your phone number."

"Here." Strollo held out a business card tucked between two of his fingers.

Samantha picked out the card, set it on her pad, and copied his contact information.

Strollo watched as she wrote, observing every detail when she leaned over to place the card on her desk: her bronzed, immaculate complexion; short, straightened black hair with bangs; and bright red lipstick. "Ms. Ayres, I have to ask you one more question. Are there any racial conflicts here?"

"What do you mean?" she asked.

"Any minorities feeling discriminated against...employees who have racist opinions causing conflicts...that kinda thing."

"We get complaints once in a while, nothing serious. We follow up on all of them. Discrimination in the workplace is against the law, so we're all over it." Samantha studied this man. She looked beyond his shirt, in dire need of pressing, and shoes looking as if they came from the Goodwill store on Briggs Lake Avenue. *This guy looks a bit disheveled, yet there's something special about him.*

"We think the Lakeside murder may have been motivated by racism—a hate crime pure and simple. Nothing appears to have been taken from Manuel Dominguez or his taxi. He had no enemies—we can't figure out why anyone would want him dead."

He took a closer look at the symmetry of her eyes, noticing the rich brown color and oval shape. He thought her Angelina Jolie lips seemed on the verge of an erupting smile.

"Very puzzling indeed," Samantha agreed.

"That's for sure, but I'll solve it."

"I'm sure you will, Detective Strollo. You look like the kind of man who knows how to get to the bottom of things."

"I've had a lot of practice."

"I'll bet you have."

"That's all I have for now. Nice meeting you, Ms. Ayres."

"You too, Detective Strollo."

"You have my number."

"And you have mine."

Strollo got up to leave, and Samantha rose from her chair. They looked into each other's eyes for a few seconds before smiling in unison, neither daring to risk another handshake.

"Thank you for your time, Ms. Ayres."

"You're welcome. Good day, Detective Strollo."

Chapter 4

TAKEDOWN

Two days later, first thing in the morning, Carl Pickler entered Samantha's office. "You wanted to see me, Samantha?"

"Yes, Carl. Thanks for coming." Samantha directed him to a nearby chair.

Pickler noticed her somber tone and that she called him "Carl" instead of "Pick"—two bad signs. "No problem." After sitting down, Pickler saw Jocko Moore in the corner of the room by the window—another bad omen. "Hi, Jocko."

"Hi, Pick." Jocko got up and joined Samantha, and they sat down at the same time in chairs opposite the young news anchor.

The office was dimly lit and so quiet, Pickler thought if someone didn't speak soon he'd be able to hear the plants growing. After what seemed to him an eternity, Samantha spoke first.

"I've concluded my investigation of the anonymous letter and—"

"—and you've decided I'm a good guy after all." Pickler finished her sentence the way he hoped she would, adding a nervous laugh.

"No. This is serious, Carl," Samantha said. "There are several instances where your comments have been extremely inappropriate. Witnesses have heard you make racially bigoted comments that are disturbing and totally unacceptable. People witnessed you using the N-word and saying you would undermine any black news anchor."

Pickler straightened up, tilted his head up, and stopped smiling. "Those are lies. I never said those things."

"To make matters worse, the *Canyon Times* will be going with a major story on its front page about alleged racism at Briggs News 20. Flip Connors has witnesses against you."

Pickler's hands trembled, so he sat on them. "Samantha... honestly...this is all bogus. You know me...anyone who knows me, knows it's not true. I'm no racist. Why would I risk my career, my reputation, and, most important, my family to say stupid things like that?"

Ignoring his question, Samantha continued. "The paper's interviewed several employees who spoke to the reporter anonymously. They intend to publish their quotes as part of the story. When you add them to the letter threatening a lawsuit and eyewitnesses backing up the allegations, it looks real bad for you." Samantha pressed her fingertips on both hands together into the shape of a church steeple. "Why would these folks come forward if they didn't have valid concerns?"

"To answer your question, anyone who would benefit from my downfall would be motivated to do this to me. If I knew who these folks were, I could be more specific," Pickler said.

"They wish to remain anonymous, and I promised to respect their confidentiality. That's only fair."

"Fair? How fair is it to me? Only a coward sends anonymous letters." Pickler squeezed the armrests on his chair until his hands turned white. Then he bit his lower lip to stop himself from saying something he might regret.

Samantha looked over at Jocko, who took the cue. "Look, Pick, this stinks. No one feels any worse about it than I do. I can imagine how you must feel too, but I have to look out for the station and its shareholders. You know I answer to a board of directors and—"

"Jocko, tell the board the kind of guy I am. You know me. You know I'm not like that."

"I don't have much choice. Look, Pick—there's no easy way to say this—the board has asked me to terminate you. They believe you have violated the personal conduct clause of your contract. I'm sorry. I hate to do it, but this is in the best interests of the station and I think for you in the long run. If this mess continues, no one wins. It could get real ugly before it's over."

Pickler gasped. "I can't believe this!" He looked out the window, but his thoughts were on his beloved wife, Marlene, and their baby boy, Cooper.

"Carl, we'd like to give you the opportunity to resign." Samantha spoke in a low and steady tone of voice. "If you resign now, this all goes away: no lawsuit, no internal investigation, only one article likely buried in the twenty-four-hour news cycle."

"Yeah, or I can lawyer up and fight for my job and reputation and not allow anonymous enemies to destroy me. I can sue for defamation of character and wrongful termination."

Jocko nodded. "You're welcome to get an attorney. Please understand if we go to court, there will be public disclosure of the letter and Samantha's investigation."

Samantha added, "It's tough to win a defamation of character suit. Remember, being a newscaster makes you a public figure. And even if you win the case, you would lose in the court of public opinion. The negative publicity could damage your reputation beyond repair in Briggs Lake. You'd never work in TV again—but that's up to you."

Pickler let out a big sigh as he exhaled. He slumped down in his chair, looking at the floor. Then he gave words to the message his body language had already spoken. "You have my resignation."

The tension lifted and calm returned to the room. No one spoke. No one moved. Jocko stared out the window. Pickler sat with his head in his hands. Samantha watched Pickler, and memories of their years working together flashed through her mind like a bittersweet highlight reel.

"You can leave for the rest of the day," Samantha said. "E-mail us your resignation letter and we'll arrange for someone to meet you on Saturday so you can clean out your desk. I'm sorry it came to this, Carl—I'm truly sorry."

"Yeah, so am I."

—ɯ—

"Anyone seen Pick?" asked the floor director as he walked through the studio.

"Nope." said one of the production techs, looking up from his camera.

"Check with Whitherspoon!" someone yelled from his table in the back of the studio without looking up from his task of organizing wireless mics.

"Can't, he's in with Jocko."

"Why do you wanna know?" the tech asked.

"'Cause he ordered four pizzas for the crew tonight. I wanted to thank him."

"What a guy! Where are they?" The tech abandoned his camera adjustments.

"The crew lounge; help yourself."

Twelve ravenous production techs materialized out of nowhere and filled the crew lounge. They were as excited as a bunch of nursing puppies at mealtime. They had twenty minutes before the preproduction meeting for the evening newscast and were taking full advantage of the unexpected snack when Jocko Moore entered, followed by Thomas Whitherspoon. Both looked as if they had returned from a funeral.

Jocko scanned the small room and saw faces intent on munching cheese, meat, and crust. The aroma of pizza saturated the air. "Say, where'd you guys get all the pizzas?" Jocko asked.

"Pick!" three techs replied simultaneously.

Jocko shrugged and rolled his eyes. "Listen up, everyone, I got an announcement. Pick resigned, so we'll run with a single anchor newscast until further notice."

Someone interrupted a collective groan from the crew. "What happened with Pick?"

"I dunno what's going on with Pick." Jocko shrugged. "Let's move on. We all have a job to do."

Jocko noticed the techs had slowed their chewing and bowed their heads. A sense of gloom descended on the lounge, making everyone go into slow motion. "That's all I have for now. Have a great newscast." He walked out.

Whitherspoon stepped to the center of the room. "Hey, guys. I'm not going anywhere. I suggested to Jocko I could do the single-anchor format permanently. I don't need a coanchor anyway. Jocko's gonna think about it."

The crew, sitting among empty pizza boxes, remained silent. Most sat still, stared at the floor, avoiding eye contact, and finished eating their pizza slices.

"This will give us a chance to redo the newscast. I've got a lot of new ideas to improve it, to give it more sizzle," Whitherspoon continued.

"Hey, Kingpin, do you know what's going on with Pick?" The director asked the question on everyone's mind.

"Don't know anything about Pick. He'll be OK. Now, getting back to my ideas. I want the show to have a fresher look. Does anyone have any creative suggestions?"

Silence.

"OK, see you at the preproduction meeting." Whitherspoon left and everyone remained silent until he had walked out of earshot.

—⁂—

That night at Hoochy's Bar and Grill, Leon Rump lifted a bottle of beer. "Let's have a toast. Long live the Kingpin."

Whitherspoon tapped his glass to Rump's bottle and took a long swig. "We did it, Leon—we got rid of Pickler, that lightweight. What a great feeling."

Their server, Trixie-Lee, delivered their food, and Rump dived into an order of wings with the gusto of a vulture that had come upon road kill. He held his fork in front of his face. "I'm looking out for ya, Kingpin. I got your back." Crumbs flicked out of his mouth and onto the table in front of him as he spoke.

"Can't believe all you've done. You gave the story about Pick using the N-word to Samantha, bribed the intern, and even drove the money to her school in Tempe."

"Least I can do, Kingpin. You're the man." Rump smiled, revealing large chunks of food in his teeth.

"Don't know what to say, but thanks, Leon."

"You're the big dog around here, baby!"

Whitherspoon smiled. Flattery and praise were the tonics for everything that ailed him. He escaped to the refuge of a mirror on a nearby wall where he could admire himself and avoid the ringside view of chicken bits decorating Rump's teeth and the mounting pile of small bones accumulating on the table.

Trixie-Lee returned and cleared dishes from the table. She always looked as if she had just climbed off her Harley-Davidson. Folks said she never wore a helmet—she didn't want to flatten her flowing black hair that she wore in a long braid. Trixie-Lee wore tight jeans and even tighter blouses to give the proper definition to her bosomy profile. Women criticized her silicone-enhanced figure, but men didn't care how it got there—they just liked the view. She seemed to have a perpetual tan, and her sleeveless tops revealed arms that had pumped a lot of iron. The ink designs adorning them would have impressed even Michelangelo.

Whitherspoon gave her a leering look. "Hey, Trixie-Lee, love your tats."

"Finally getting around to noticing my body art?"

"I've been noticing your body art for years. I think I could bounce a quarter a foot off your ass. Waddya say we give it a try?"

"You'll have to catch me first."

"Speaking of your behind, I got another idea: get a new tattoo—one right across your butt—that says 'The Kingpin.'"

She put both hands on her hips. "Yeah, that's a pretty good idea, Kingpin. I'll be sure to run that by my boyfriend tonight when I get home."

"Good. Say, how's my hair looking? I try to look my best for you."

"That's your hair? I thought you wore a rug."

"It's the real deal, all right. You're welcome to run your fingers through it anytime you want."

"Good to know. I'll keep that in mind."

—⁓—

At the Pickler home, Carl attempted to console Marlene. He held his sobbing and shaking wife close as he told her about the meeting with Jocko and Samantha. "It doesn't bother me because I know it's not true. I'm not a racist. People who know me know that."

"What're we going to do?" She looked up at him, her eyes full of tears.

"I'll get another job, honey. We'll be OK." His voice calm, his touch tender, he massaged her back lightly to emphasize that last point. He set his chin on her head to keep her from seeing the tears welling up in his own eyes. Pickler smelled the lavender from Marlene's shampoo and the warmth from her body. *I love this woman.*

"Why don't you call Kingpin—see what he can do. Either he knows what went down, or he can help you get another job."

"I'm planning on it. Mr. Whitherspoon is one of my strongest allies, and I know he'll do anything he can to help me."

The following day the front-page headline read, "Briggs News 20 Anchor Resigns Amid Racism Claims." Jocko Moore settled in his desk chair, coffee cup in hand, and studied every word. He took a breath and called Samantha Ayres. "Hey, I just read it.

Coulda been a whole lot worse. There were more innuendos than facts."

"Yeah, I thought the same thing. All their sources were anonymous, and the quotes read like gossip. I think we've dodged a bullet."

"I guess we'll have to wait and see what happens, but if the story doesn't have legs, this could all go away." He sighed.

"Could be, we'll have to see how it plays out," Samantha said.

"If they contact me for my reaction, I'll just say Pick resigned for personal reasons."

"Legal approved those talking points, Jocko, so if you stick to them, you'll be fine."

"Samantha, if it turns out the charges are bogus, we may look back on this and conclude we pulled the trigger too soon on Pick."

"We had no choice. We had to act on the information we were given and what we thought to be true at the time. We could still have exposure to discrimination or hostile workplace lawsuits before this is over," Samantha said.

"You might be right. But if a few anonymous employees, and an intern, can take down a man like Carl Pickler—we got some big problems somewhere. Find 'em and fix 'em before this kind of garbage blows up in our face again. You own this, Samantha. Do you understand?" He set his cup down on the desk so hard she could hear it on her cell phone.

"Yes, Jocko." Samantha pushed her fingers up and down on her forehead.

Chapter 5

KINGPIN SEES THE LIGHT

The kitchen phone rang, so she picked it up.

"Hello. Mrs. Pickler?"

"Yes."

"My name's Leon Rump. I'm the chief engineer at Briggs News 20. I used to work with your husband. I wanna say how sorry I am for what happened to him. Is he there?"

"He's unavailable. Can I take a message?" Still wearing her robe and pajamas, she stretched for a pen from a kitchen drawer.

"No. That's OK. You're the one I wanted to talk to anyway. What happened to your husband—it was a setup by Tom Whitherspoon."

"That's a shocker. Why?" She squinted and clenched her teeth, bracing for his answer.

"Whitherspoon's jealous of your husband, wanted him out of the way, so he bad-mouthed him every chance he got. I stuck up for him the best I could."

"That's hard to believe. Carl has always spoken so highly of Mr. Whitherspoon."

"I know. It bothered me to see the way your husband looked up to the guy who, I knew for a fact, stabbed him in the back."

"My husband thinks Mr. Whitherspoon is his mentor."

"Just the opposite—his biggest enemy. Sorry to have to tell you that."

"Why are you telling me this?"

"Felt you should know the truth," Rump replied.

"OK. Thanks...I think." She sighed and dropped onto a nearby stool.

"Look, I wanna help you, Mrs. Pickler. Maybe we could meet sometime for lunch or dinner. You and I—let's keep your husband out of this. I can share more details then and let you know what's going on at the station."

"I don't know if I should. My husband wouldn't like me going out with another man."

"He doesn't need to know. It'll be our little secret."

Marlene looked down at her wedding ring and straightened it on her finger. She pulled her robe closer and tightened the knot around her waist. "I don't know about that, Mr. Rump."

"It's for his own good. Don't you want to help your husband?"

"Sure, but—"

"I'll give you my number. Call me when you can get away. We'll meet, put our heads together, and see what we can do for Carl."

Marlene took down his number and hung up. She slammed the pen down on the kitchen counter. She wanted to find out what happened at the station, and this guy could provide a lot of information. But he wanted secrecy. Not in the habit of keeping anything from Carl, she weighed the pros and cons. Should she meet with this stranger and keep it from her husband?

At that moment Carl came through the front door carrying Cooper.

She jumped to her feet. "Oh—you scared me."

"It's just me and Cooper."

"How was the walk, honey?"

"Wonderful. Loved the fresh air, and the birds serenaded us the whole time. Cooper slept while I pushed his carriage through the park and got some thinking done."

"What about?" she asked.

"Things."

"What do you mean 'things'?"

"Just things," he said.

"Got a call from a Leon Rump. Says he's the chief engineer?"

"What'd he want? Do I need to call him back?"

"No, he didn't want a call back; he wanted to say he's sorry about what happened."

"That's nice of him."

"He had another piece of news."

"What?"

"He said Tom Whitherspoon orchestrated the conspiracy against you."

"Why would he do that?"

"Because he's jealous, according to Mr. Rump. Come to think of it, I didn't like the way Whitherspoon stole that murder story out from under you. I thought at the time he was afraid you were getting too popular with the viewers and decided to protect his turf."

"Well, Whitherspoon doesn't have anything to worry about now."

—⁜—

Pickler was wrong. That evening, while driving home from the studio, Thomas Whitherspoon felt queasy. Shooting pains throbbed up and down his left arm. *I'm having a heart attack,* he thought. Ten minutes away from his gated community, he decided to keep driving. When he arrived home, the pain seemed to go away. *Just tired. That's all.*

Whitherspoon dropped his suit coat on a chair, got a pitcher of ice water from the refrigerator, filled a glass, and gulped it down. He kicked off his shoes and loosened his tie. The recliner beckoned. He dropped himself on it, leaned back, and turned on the TV from the remote on the armrest. Whitherspoon liked to TiVo the newscast so he could watch himself before going to bed.

The throbbing in his left arm returned. Something pressed against his chest, making breathing difficult; perspiration seeped from every pore. The pangs came in waves, and each time they returned stronger. When the pain and panic distracted him from viewing himself on the newscast, he knew it was time to call 9-1-1.

Whitherspoon leaned forward and reached for his phone. His arm hurt and he shivered as his body collapsed to the floor. The phone bounced out of reach; he couldn't move. *Oh my God, I'm afraid of dying! I should've taken care of myself. What if the EMTs find my porn? Oh, God! God, I don't want to die! Please don't let me die. I'll change. I'll do good things. I promise...please...give me a second chance.*

Whitherspoon rolled on his back. He saw a bright column of light growing brighter and wider every second from the floor to the ceiling. Its jagged flames looked like fire but without heat. He stared at the beam of light until going numb. Fear and pain left, replaced by a feeling of well-being. His muscles relaxed as if he was in a hot tub. He heard music and smelled the aroma of fresh flowers in full bloom. *This must be what death feels like: ecstasy.* Then he passed out.

—⚏—

The next morning, Whitherspoon awoke and opened one eye, then the other. Lying on his side on the living room floor, he could see the sun shining through the windows. *I'm alive! I got a second chance.*

He hadn't felt so good in years. *Did last night really happen? Did I make a deal with God—or was it the devil? Or did I imagine the whole thing?* He poured a glass of orange juice then found the place in the carpet where the column of light had risen like a fountain. It showed no evidence of the previous night's light show.

Whitherspoon took a hot shower as ideas bombarded him. He could help Pickler get a job, support Detective Strollo's homicide investigation, give money to charity, and promote community outreach programs. When he got the idea to call his ex-wife to say he was sorry for ruining their marriage, he decided he'd gone too far and should stop this kind of thinking before he did something he would regret later.

He dressed and drove to work. As Whitherspoon approached the concrete steps of Briggs News 20's studio, he saw a panhandler. "Here, take twenty dollars. Buy yourself a good meal."

"Thank you, sir!" The ragged man gaped in astonishment.

"You're welcome, sir." Whitherspoon bounded up the steps to the office building of the TV station, two at a time. Once inside, he marched toward his cubicle and saw his producer. "Hi, Carol, how are you?"

"Fine. What's with you?"

"I've never felt so good in my life!" He looked at the empty cubicles in the newsroom. "Where is everyone? Did your annoying personality drive everyone out of here?"

"They're at mandatory safety training in the studio."

"Why aren't you there? Are you banned from attending meetings?"

Carol pushed her chair out from the desk and grinned from ear to ear. "I'm working on a special project for Samantha, proofing her quarterly EEO report."

"That's great. I'm so happy to see you supporting the rest of the team for once."

"Yeah, right. We both know I'm allowed to help others only when *you're* not around."

He smiled. "Glad you know your priorities in life. Kingpin first, everyone else second...but not for too long."

"You seem so happy, boss. Did you decide to move out of Crabby Town?"

"What are you talking about? My cheerful presence is uplifting and brings joy to those around me, like a beacon of light."

"Yeah, sort of a like a black light. You even make things glow in the dark."

"Enough, Lackey!" he shouted, but couldn't keep from laughing afterward. "Look, Miss Witty, get your jollies picking on someone from your own intellectual level and leave brilliant thinkers like me alone." He set his briefcase in his chair but remained standing. "I got an idea. Why don't we do more positive and inspiring stories? It could jack up ratings."

"Now you sound like you moved from Crabby Town to Fantasy Island. You know the drill. Feel-good stories are nice, but they don't drive ratings. People love bad news: deaths, scandals, rapes, and violence—that kinda stuff." She took a rubber band, stretched it back, and took a shot at his head, missing it by inches. "You're slipping in your old age."

"Watch it, lady, or I'll report you to Samantha for creating a hostile workplace." He wagged his finger at her.

"*You* are a walking, talking hostile workplace."

"I'm serious, Carol. We aren't doing a good job covering inspirational stories. First, we gotta get excited ourselves and then commit to producing compelling programming that will engage viewers."

"Are you smoking something? Crimes get eyeballs, eyeballs get ratings, and ratings get ad dollars. That's how we make those big bucks. Correction, that's how *you* make those big bucks."

"Carol, I want to make a difference—a positive difference."

"You *are* serious, aren't you?" She clutched her notebook and pen, jotting notes as the ideas came to her. "OK. Let's see...feel-good story ideas...We could ask viewers to recommend stories about the positive things going on around town. We reward the best idea each week by covering the story and featuring it on the evening news."

Whitherspoon finished her thought. "Yeah, then we enter each week's winner in a contest. After three months we choose a winner from all the weekly stories and do a special on-air presentation during my newscast."

"The station could make a donation to their favorite charity," she added.

"Now you're talking. Work on that. I've got a meeting with someone special."

"Who? Did you finally find a girlfriend who loved you as much as you love yourself?"

"Not yet. Please watch my briefcase and work on that idea while I'm gone."

"What else is new? You come up with the ideas and I do all the work."

"But don't I give you all the credit?" He smiled and walked toward the door.

"Actually, you don't. But I'd rather have more money—keep that in mind. OK, go." She held out her pencil toward him. "But do me one favor."

He stopped and looked at her. "What?"

"Try not to frighten small children."

—◊—

The Golf Shack served good breakfasts, and golfers loved to indulge in the cuisine before and after a round on the public course. The cook, Benny Joseph, retired to Arizona from working as a chef in large New York City restaurants. He still loved to cook, so he worked at the Shack in the mornings. The golfers were the beneficiaries of his continued culinary passion, and they appreciated the value they received from their superstar chef.

Besides the good food for a fair price, Marlene Pickler chose to meet Leon Rump at the Shack because her husband disliked golf, so there would be no chance of running into him.

"Cool place, Marlene. You don't mind if I call you Marlene, do you?"

"No." Marlene's gaze shifted from table to table, making sure she didn't recognize anyone.

"You're looking hot today." Rump slurped his coffee. "If I didn't know you'd just recently had a baby, I couldn't tell by looking at your body."

"Thanks. But we're here to talk about my husband. What can you tell me about what went down at the station?"

Rump pulled at his ponytail and gave an expression he thought would make her think him deep in thought. "When Pick, I mean Carl, got raves and complimentary comments from viewers, I noticed Kingpin getting jealous."

"What'd he say?"

"Don't recall the details, but he got critical, always said bad stuff about how he worked on-air."

Marlene adjusted her silverware. "Did Jocko Moore intervene or stick up for my husband? Why would he allow it?"

"Don't know. Can't say for sure. Never had much dealings with Jocko." Rump took another sip of coffee, and a slight amount dripped off his chin, causing Marlene to look out the window at the tee. "Your hair looks great. I've always preferred blonds."

"Ah, thanks. What does the staff think about Carl's sudden departure? Do they know about the accusations?"

"The staff loves him—always have. They wonder why he left without saying good-bye, which I think was a big mistake."

"Carl was told to leave the building right away and not talk to anyone."

"That explains that. But still, he didn't fight for his job. I would've if I was married to someone cute like you—to keep those paychecks coming in. That's what real men do. Just sayin'."

"He must have his reasons."

"Are your eyes blue or green? I can't tell."

"Let's keep it on the subject at hand. Would you speak with my husband and see if you can talk him into going back and meeting with Jocko and explaining himself and try to get his job back?"

"I'll think about it. Not sure it would do any good. He's stubborn. You probably know that."

"My husband's a good man."

"I'm sure he is. He just didn't seem to have the stomach to fight for his job. Kinda wimped out on you. That's all I'm saying." Rump tugged at his shirt collar. "I'm just sorry he didn't take care of his woman like he should have. You deserve better, Marlene."

She looked out the window, trying to think of something to say. Before she knew it, she felt something on her leg. Rump was stroking her under the table with his fingertips. She gasped. "Shit!" She picked up her coffee cup and tossed the contents in his face. "You lowlife, dumb ass, son of a bitch!"

Marlene stormed out of the Shack as every eye turned to Rump, who sat stunned, coffee dripping from his chin to the tabletop.

—∞—

The next morning, she entered her kitchen wearing a yellow cotton bathrobe, her blond hair unkempt and dark circles under her eyes. She glanced at her husband who sat in a trance-like state at the kitchen table, his empty cereal bowl pushed in front of him, intently working on the newspaper's crossword puzzle.

"I finally got Cooper down. Hopefully he'll sleep for a while. I wish I could sleep. He kept me up all night." Marlene shuffled toward the coffeepot, poured a cup, and spilled coffee on the kitchen counter. "Shit!"

"That's nice," He said without looking up.

"What's nice? That he kept me up all night, or that I said shit?" Marlene turned her back on him, wiped the counter, then climbed onto a stool and looked down at her husband. "Dude, you weren't even listening were you?"

"No—I mean yeah," he said, still looking down at the puzzle.

"Hey. I'm talking to you. What's more important, me or that stupid crossword?"

He looked up, pencil in hand, his eye brows knitted. "You are."

"Good choice! Now, pay attention—the questions are going to get harder. I wanna talk while we have the chance." Holding the cup in both hands, she took a sip of coffee then set it down on the counter behind her.

"About what?" He scowled.

"How could you let all that crap happen to you at work? The guy I married was smart, he was tough, and he was fearless."

"And your point is?"

"What the hell happened? You let Whitherspoon, Samantha, and Jocko blindside you. You let them destroy your career. They ambushed you and you fell apart like a piece of wet toilet paper." She tightened her jaw and frowned.

"What do you want me to say?" He fixed his eyes on hers.

"I want to know what you were thinking." Her face flashed with anger.

After a few seconds, he looked at his crossword to escape her glare.

"Wait. I'm still talking." She jumped off the stool, snatched the pencil from his hand, and slammed it on the kitchen table. "We're not done yet!"

"What's your problem?" He jumped to his feet and braced for a fight, trying to look as dignified as a man could while wearing a food-stained t-shirt and striped boxer shorts.

She jabbed him in the chest with her forefinger to emphasize each word. "You're so clueless, it's embarrassing."

He exploded. "Oh, that's great. Keep insulting me—just what I need now."

Marlene scolded. "Lower your voice! The baby's sleeping."

"Look. I knew what was going on. Whitherspoon felt threatened and undermined me every chance he got." He sighed. "I was disappointed, but what could I do?"

"Why didn't you fight back instead of acting like such a naive dumb ass?" she said.

"Oh, how feminine!" His face flushed. "Your cursing and name-calling is a real turn-on. Sure doesn't sound like the sweet girl I married—more like an inmate in a women's prison."

"Don't change the subject. We're talking about you. Even Mr. Rump noticed how Whitherspoon treated you and couldn't figure out why you kept kissing Kingpin's ass."

"Did Rump say that?" The veins popped out in his temples.

"Basically," Marlene said.

"How'd he get involved in this anyway? Boy, you and Rump sure got cozy all of a sudden!"

"He called to offer *us* help, remember?"

"It's weird that out of the blue he wants to be your new best friend, but when we worked together he never gave me the time of day."

"Are you jealous?"

"Of what?"

"You said you knew what was going on, but I don't think you knew the extent of Whitherspoon's undermining. You're clueless."

"When I comprehended the fact that he thwarted my career advancement at every opportunity, I went to Jocko."

"And Jocko didn't do a damned thing, did he?"

"Jocko advised me to avoid conflict, keep being a team player, and let my work speak for itself. He said down the road, my time would come."

"Well that strategy sure worked *great,* didn't it?" She turned to the kitchen counter, took a gulp of her coffee, and climbed back on the stool.

"It did work. When I anchored the news alone, my ratings were comparable to our joint newscasts. Surveys showed the eighteen-to-thirty-five demographic preferred me to Whitherspoon. Jocko assured me it would only be a matter of time until I got my break."

He leaned against the kitchen table, resting his palms on its edge, and gauged his wife's reaction to these revelations.

"OK, fine. You played dumb and took the high road...So when the shit hit the fan, why didn't you fight for yourself, instead of rolling over and acting like a pansy-ass? You should have sued those bastards."

"I considered taking them to court—didn't know all they had on me, but Jocko seemed to think they had a solid case. He said if I sued them he'd reveal details that would embarrass our family. If I called his bluff, litigated, and won—which wasn't necessarily a slam dunk—the media would still have a feeding frenzy.

And assuming I got my old job back—where would I go to get my reputation back?"

"So why in the world didn't you let me know what you were doing? I thought we were a team—best friends. That really hurts."

"I wanted to protect you. Your pregnancy was rough, and you were sick all the time. I thought it best to shield you from the extra stress. I figured if I shared the drama at work, it would freak you out."

"Well, here's a news flash, buddy—I'm freaked out—big-time!"

"Sorry." He studied the floor. "I did it out of love for you. That's all I can say."

Marlene trembled and burst into tears that edged down her face, making wet streaks. He leaned over and wrapped his arms around her. She slid off the stool to return his embrace. One of her slippers fell off, so she kicked off the other one.

Holding her, he rocked her back and forth. "It's OK, honey. We'll get through this." He kissed her. "You need to go back to bed and get some sleep."

She locked her arms around his neck and squeezed her body against his until her robe came undone.

He lifted Marlene in his arms and cradled her to their bedroom.

—⁂—

Two hours later, Marlene answered a knock at the door. It was Thomas Whitherspoon.

"Hi, Marlene. May I speak to Carl for a few minutes?"

"Mr. Whitherspoon, come in." She opened the front door wider while holding her baby son, Cooper, in her left arm. Wearing black shorts and a pink blouse, her hair still wet from a shower, Marlene's porcelain skin radiated a glow that lit the room. "I'll get him. He's showering. We got up early then both took a nap. Please sit down." She motioned toward the kitchen table and left saying, "I've got to feed Cooper."

Whitherspoon looked around the kitchen. Magnets stuck to the refrigerator with inspirational slogans. One that caught his attention proclaimed, "I can do all things." A granite countertop encircled the kitchen's copper sink and shiny, clean stainless steel stove. Walls decorated with small speckled stars were adorned with artwork; skylights ushered in beams of sunlight, which shimmered on the floor. He smelled cinnamon and freshly brewed coffee.

"Hi, Tom. What brings you here?" Pickler extended his hand as he walked into the kitchen.

"We need to talk," Whitherspoon said. "I'm sorry about what happened. I want to help." He opened his jacket and moved his chair farther from the table.

Pickler sat at the table opposite his visitor. A spot of white shaving cream on his ear, his blue eyes bored into Whitherspoon's

"Why do you want to help me *now*? Kind of late for that. Are you feeling guilty about something?" Pickler stared.

"What are you talking about?"

"I've heard from reliable sources you were behind the lies that got me fired." Pickler's firm tone revealed no trace of anger.

"Me?" Whitherspoon cleared his throat and placed his palm on his chest. "That's crazy talk. I didn't say anything about you. Besides, I heard you up and quit."

"Yeah, right. I quit. They were going to fire me if I didn't."

"Who told you I had anything to do with it?" Whitherspoon asked.

Pickler drummed his fingernails on the tabletop. "Doesn't matter now. It's water under the bridge."

"Look, I feel terrible about what happened to you. I want to help. That's all. Do you need money, references, what?"

"I'm good. Thanks anyway, *Kingpin*," Pickler deadpanned.

Whitherspoon heard Marlene talking to her baby in the adjacent room. "Say, I'm looking forward to being Cooper's godfather. Have you scheduled his baptism yet? I'm honored—"

"We've had a change in plans. Detective Strollo will be the godfather. We didn't think you'd be appropriate under the circumstances."

"Oh, I see. OK. Strollo's a good choice—good man. Is his daughter still a star softball pitcher?"

"Yes."

Both men looked down at the tabletop in front of them. They listened to Marlene talking to Cooper as she fed him in the next room and heard his contented cooing.

Whitherspoon glanced at the half-finished crossword puzzle on the kitchen table. "You do crosswords?"

"Yep."

The kitchen clock chimed ten times. Then the room fell silent.

"Guess I should get going." Whitherspoon rose from his chair. "Let me know if you need anything."

"See you around, Kingpin." Pickler smiled at Whitherspoon and raised his arm in a brief wave.

After Whitherspoon left, Marlene scurried into the kitchen carrying the baby. "I heard everything. You were professional but didn't act like his groupie either. I wish I could have seen his face when you told him we fired him from being Cooper's godfather. His jaw must have hit the floor. You got him good."

Pickler didn't hear anything she said. He ran his right hand back and forth on the table, staring at the design, lost in thought.

—m—

After leaving the Picklers' home, Whitherspoon got into his 911 Carrera 4S Cabriolet Porsche, raised the top, and turned on the air-conditioning. He drove toward the desert. The purple and brown hues of the distant mountains glistened in the sunlight. The sand and rock passed faster with each mile. He activated his Bluetooth and called Leon Rump.

"Leon, Kingpin here. Give me a call when you get a chance. Thanks."

He drove for ten minutes waiting for a call back. When none came, he called his ex-wife. "Naomi, guess who this is?"

"Tom! Good to hear from you. It's been years. How's everything?"

"Fine. I've been thinking about us and...I want to say...I'm sorry."

"That's OK. It's in the past, eons ago." Her voice was softer and warmer than he had remembered.

Whitherspoon swallowed hard and took a deep breath. "Well, totally my fault that we didn't work out. I was a selfish jackass. Sorry for all the BS I put you through."

"Apology accepted. That's very sweet of you. I know I reacted harshly to your shenanigans. I'm sorry for that too," she said cheerfully.

"When we split, I enforced the prenup," he said. "I shouldn't have done that. Just being spiteful."

"I didn't care about the prenup. I loved you. I didn't want your money."

"I know. You're a special woman, Naomi. Not many would have handled it like that."

"That's in the past."

"Well, what about now? Can I set you up with an annuity or something? I can take care of you financially for the rest of your life. I'm prepared to do that."

"It's not necessary, Tom. I'm very comfortable, and my business is doing well."

"OK. Thought I'd ask. Say, I thought we could get together some weekend. I could fly to Denver and we could see a show, talk, and kind of catch up."

"Tom, there's something I need to tell you. I remarried last year. He's a great guy, and we're deeply in love. I've never been happier in my life."

"Oh, that's awesome. I'm happy for you. Glad I called—didn't know that. Hey, congratulations. Well, I gotta go."

"Thanks, Tom. You take good care of yourself."

"I will. Stay well. Bye now." He studied the mountains ahead of him and thought they looked like people—sad people.

Whitherspoon's cell phone jarred him back to reality.

"This is Tom Whitherspoon."

A breathless Carol Lackey blurted out. "Kingpin, come to the office quick. Jocko called a staff meeting and wants you here ASAP."

Chapter 6

JOCKO HIRES THE NEXT RISING STAR

When Whitherspoon pulled his Porsche into the Briggs News parking lot to attend Jocko's impromptu staff meeting, he saw a man with light blue eyes sitting in a lawn chair smoking a cigarette next to a shopping cart filled with blankets, coats, plastic bags, and books. A nearby sign read: "Vet. Needs food. Please help. God bless you." Whitherspoon tossed a twenty-dollar bill in his donation can.

The man smiled, revealing two missing front teeth. "Thanks. Be careful who you trust."

Startled by the warning, Whitherspoon stepped closer to the man until the smell of urine stopped him. "What'd you say?"

"I said be careful who you trust, who you open up to. Some people are out to get you." The man smiled again and nodded.

"Thanks for the tip. I'll keep that in mind. I got a tip for you. Try to get a bath worked into your busy schedule—you stink!"

Whitherspoon walked from the parking lot into the building and entered the room just as the staff meeting commenced. Reporters, producers, and photographers stood in their cubicles, their heads above the partitions like bean sprouts. The production crew members leaned against the walls, a human picket fence that encircled the room.

In the open space at the center of the room, a clean-cut man in his early thirties, with a military-style short haircut, posed like an action hero with his arms behind his back. His brown hair matched his eyes, and he wore a seersucker suit, a designer shirt, but no tie.

Jocko positioned himself next to the man and rubbed the top of his bald head, a gesture always used when he was about to say something significant. "I called this meeting to introduce you to a new employee. This is Rex Martin. He's going to coanchor the news with the Kingpin. He comes highly recommended from his last job in New Mexico." He raised his arm and held his hand toward Martin.

The staff reacted with polite applause. Several women staffers exchanged glances and brief smiles. Erin O'Haven, the weather maven, glowed. Her excitement resembled the last time she had reported on severe dust storms, a welcome relief from the tired routine of reporting on hot, sunny days. She preened, pulling strands of hair behind her ears, blinking her eyes more than usual.

Jocko pointed to Martin. "He won a local Emmy for his reports on a serial killer. I've been looking for someone of his caliber for a long time."

The women didn't hear a thing Jocko said. They fixated on this pleasant hunk of manhood, which certainly must have been a gift to them from a gracious god.

A chill cut through Whitherspoon's body like a knife. *Rex Martin. Never heard of him. I thought I knew all the major players in the broadcast industry.* Whitherspoon's heart raced. He looked at Jocko. *It sure didn't take him long to replace Pickler. It would have been nice if he'd consulted me first. What's this "looking for a long time" stuff?*

"In the next hour we'll issue a media release announcing Rex's arrival, and we'll introduce him to our viewers on tonight's newscast. You wanna say a few words, Rex?"

"Sure, Jocko." Martin stepped forward. Moving his head from side to side, he made eye contact with as many people as he could while he spoke. "I'm from New Mexico, where I anchored the news in a smaller market and did investigative reporting. I like to work out. I lift weights. I'm single and looking."

"Good-looking," Erin muttered.

The women around her giggled.

"What'd you say, Erin?" Jocko growled.

"Nothing, boss." She wiped the smile off her face with a dramatic sweeping gesture of her hand, which triggered more snickering.

Jocko nodded for Martin to continue.

"I like traveling. I'm looking forward to getting to know all of you. Thanks." He looked around with a wide smile, resting his gaze on Erin.

"Thanks, Rex. Welcome aboard. I'm expecting some big things from you." Turning to face the group in the studio, Jocko addressed them. "A reminder: we have a safety meeting tomorrow at one o'clock, so there's an early crew call. Have a great show tonight."

Jocko clutched Martin by the shoulder and turned him toward Whitherspoon. "Rex, this is Thomas Whitherspoon. He's our senior anchor. We call him the Kingpin. He's had a long and distinguished career in the news business."

Whitherspoon smiled. *For all his faults, at least Jocko understands who I am and how important I am to the station. He gets me. I have to give him that.*

Martin extended his hand and Whitherspoon shook it.

As the crew dispersed to prepare for that night's newscast, Ronnie Gaboni, the sports director, gripped Martin's hand. "I belong to the best gym in town. You can go anytime as my guest."

"I'll take you up on that," Martin said, then caught Erin's eye. Wearing her newest emerald green dress, she zigzagged through the mob of colleagues until she got near enough to extend her hand.

"Hi, I'm Erin O'Haven, the weather maven. I'm from Minnesota, but I know this town well enough to give you the grand tour when you get a chance."

"Thanks, Erin. I'd love to take you up on that." Martin grinned, revealing whitened teeth.

"All right, you guys, let's break this up. We've got to make some TV today. Rex and Tom, could I see you both in my office for a quick meeting?" Jocko motioned toward the door.

They followed Jocko down the hallway to his office, which was in its usual state of clutter. The smell of stale coffee permeated the room. The office's coveted corner location, a symbol of his power, allowed for plenty of sunshine through two windows that stretched from the floor to the ceiling. They provided a bird's-eye view of the silent traffic below. The crew called it "Jocko's perch."

Martin and Whitherspoon sat at the table, eyeing one another like boxers sizing up the competition before the opening bell.

Jocko, sweating more than usual, filled his mug from the coffeepot and held the pot toward them. "You guys want some?"

"No thanks," said Whitherspoon.

"Nope," chimed in Martin.

Jocko eased into his big leather chair at the head of the table. After a few seconds, he wiped the top of his head. "Tom, sorry I couldn't discuss this with you first. I did try to contact you. Carol said you were out of the office. I felt the need to notify the staff as soon as possible and get out a news release. Stuff like this gets around fast, and I didn't want competitors to scoop us on our own announcement."

"Not a problem," Whitherspoon's red face betrayed him. He clenched his teeth and repeatedly pressed his thumb against his forefinger in a circular motion.

At that moment, Leon Rump barged into Jocko's office and pointed both forefingers at Martin. "Just heard the news! Sorry I missed the staff meeting. I wanna congratulate the new hire. Welcome aboard."

"Thanks, Uncle Leon!" Martin stood up and they embraced.

"Why didn't you call me for a ride from the airport?" Rump asked.

Martin replied, "Oh, I didn't want to inconvenience you. I don't mind taking taxis."

"Now, Rex, make sure you take good care of the Kingpin," Rump said.

"I will, Uncle Leon!"

After nodding to Jocko and giving Whitherspoon the thumbs-up, Rump left the office and closed the door behind him.

Uncle Leon? Whitherspoon fumed. *Are you kidding me? Thank you for the heads-up, Uncle Leon! Now I know why you were so eager to help me get Pickler out of the way. You were angling to get your nephew a job!* He nodded at Martin and smiled. "I also want to welcome you aboard, Rex. I'm sure we'll be a great team."

"I agree," Jocko said. "I've waited for an opportunity to get someone like Rex on the team. He got our attention when the ratings of his station went through the roof. His reports on a serial killer in New Mexico showed me he's a rising star in our industry."

Rising star, my ass, Whitherspoon thought. "Did they ever catch the killer?"

"Not yet," Martin replied and turned his attention to Jocko.

Jocko continued. "I wanted us to meet for a few minutes and talk about our vision for the newscast."

"Glad you mentioned vision, Jocko. I've got an idea that will bring in viewers and create some excitement," Whitherspoon said. "Instead of focusing solely on crimes and disasters during our evening newscasts, let's make an effort to cover some 'feel-good' stories."

Jocko got up and looked out the window. "You know those stories don't attract viewers the way rapes, murders, and other crimes do. If we had a serial killer on the loose, our ratings would go sky high. I know it's cynical, but that's the world we live in."

"I know, but—"

"That's reality, Tom."

"I know, Jocko. One solitary, positive story each week, that's all I'm suggesting. Not go overboard. Make a viewer contest out of it to keep them tuned in. After three months we let our viewers choose the grand-prize winner and give them a ten-thousand-dollar prize we can take from the marketing budget. It'll generate some hoopla and could jack up ratings."

Jocko turned away from the window and back to his coan-chors. "What do you think, Rex?"

"With all due respect to Mr. Whitherspoon, I think it's a bad idea, Mr. Moore. I got our market share up ten points by reporting on crime and hard news—not puff pieces." Martin looked down and picked some lint off his pant leg and flicked it on the floor as though it was Whitherspoon's idea.

Jocko's phone rang. "OK, I'll be right there." Putting down the phone, he said, "Guys, I got a fire to put out. Introduce Rex on the newscast tonight, Tom. You can try out your idea, and we'll see how it works. To be honest, I'm not expecting much."

Whitherspoon left Jocko's office in search of Leon Rump. *He's got some explaining to do!*

—⚏—

The gloomy lighting in Strollo's office, enhanced by the old-fashioned desk lamp, revealed a day-old tuna sandwich aban-doned on a bookshelf. The detective tapped his pen on the gray metallic desktop to the tune of a '60s rock 'n' roll song playing on his oldies station. *Why would someone stab a cab driver and club him to death but not rob him? It makes no sense.*

The phone rang.

"Strollo."

"Daddy! Guess what? Arizona State's head coach is coming to scout me in a couple of weeks and wants to meet with us after the game. Can you be there?"

"It depends on my work, sweetheart. I'll try."

"Let's plan on you being there, OK? This is a big deal," she said.

"I know, Hannah. I'll do everything I can to make it. Are you home now?"

"No, I'm at school. Thought I should call before softball practice."

"OK. Thanks. I'll be home late, so go ahead and eat dinner without me. Love you."

"Love you too, Daddy. Bye-bye."

—⁂—

That evening, the six o'clock newscast began with a tight headshot of Whitherspoon. "My new coanchor comes to us from a New Mexico TV station. He has a degree from the University of New Mexico in broadcasting and has won a local Emmy. Please welcome Rex Martin!"

The cameras switched to a wide-angle shot of the news desk. "Thanks, Tom. I'm pleased to be a part of the Briggs News 20 team. We're going to give you the news you want to hear because we want you to 'Hear It Here First!'"

"That's right, Rex. 'Hear It Here First!' isn't a catchphrase. It's the way we operate, and it's in our DNA."

The director switched back to a close-up of Whitherspoon, who looked into the camera. "That's why tonight we're launching a contest. We want our viewers to uncover uplifting stories about local, unsung heroes and submit them to viewers@BriggsLakenews. com. Each week we'll select a winner and report on that story during Friday's newscast. We'll call it 'The Good News Show.'"

The director switched to a different camera. Whitherspoon picked up the cue and turned his head to the second camera. "After three months, viewers will vote for the most inspirational story. We'll feature the grand-prize winner live on a newscast and present a ten-thousand-dollar check."

The newscast continued with Erin O'Haven forecasting more sunny weather tomorrow and the "Insider's Report on Sports" from Ronnie Gaboni about the Arizona Diamondbacks. At the close of the broadcast, e-mail messages with ideas for "The Good News Show" had already begun filling the station's inbox.

Whitherspoon signed off. "Thanks for watching, and remember, 'Hear It Here First!'" The cameras switched to the wide-angle shot as their mics were cut. The volume of the show's theme music came up.

The floor director counted out the show. "Three...two...one...clear...we're out!"

An audio tech removed Whitherspoon's mic pack, then Martin's. "Good show, guys. You did well for the first time, Rex." The tech paused, impressed with the newscaster's bulked-up chest and arms. "I can sure tell you like lifting weights. You wouldn't have needed to say anything at the meeting."

"Thanks. Yeah, I try to make it to the gym six days a week. I alternate muscle groups so I work them every other day." Martin looked at Whitherspoon. "Hey, Kingpin, wanna go out for a drink?"

"Can't tonight, Rex. Sorry. I've been trying to get with your Uncle Leon all day since our morning meeting. We have some things to discuss." Whitherspoon removed his earpiece, placed it in its carrying case, and raced to Leon Rump's workshop in the back of the building.

Ronnie and Erin came over to the news desk to congratulate Martin on his first night. "We'll take you up on your offer," Erin said.

Martin nodded. Turning to the crew, he raised his voice so all could hear. "Anyone else want to go out for a drink with us? I'm treating."

The audio tech, a cameraman, and teleprompter operator took him up on his offer, and they huddled for a quick discussion on the various options this time of night as they exited the door to the rear parking lot. Martin's gesture of goodwill meant a lot—even to those who couldn't go. Whitherspoon had never invited them out. They had a good first impression of the new guy, who in his first night on the job treated them as equals.

—⁊⁊—

Leon Rump's workshop contained shelves of microphones, tripods, recording decks, and spools of multicolored wiring. The long workbench displayed equipment torn apart in the process of repair. Rump presided over his electronic jungle perched on a stool, looking like the Lion King while holding a Philly cheese steak in both hands. "I liked the newscast tonight, Kingpin! You and Rex make a great team!"

"Why didn't you tell me you were trying to get your nephew a job at the station?"

"I dunno. Didn't want to bother you with it, I guess," Rump replied. "Say, your hair looked real good on the show tonight. You doing something different with it?"

"As a matter of fact, I had it trimmed and changed the tint. Glad you liked it—going for a youthful look. Hope the viewers like it, too."

"They'll *love* it!" Rump gushed.

"Thanks. You don't miss a thing, Leon. Anyway, I distinctly recall asking why you were going to such lengths to help me get rid of Pickler, and you led me to believe your only motivation was to support me."

"I was—*am* supporting you. Look, I didn't like the way Pickler badmouthed you and tried to take you down." Rump set the half-eaten sandwich on the workbench and wiped his hands on his jeans.

"Yeah, but you were mainly working to get Pickler out so you could bring your nephew in—so *he* could replace Pickler as our rising star. Right?"

"That's part of it, but not all of it," Rump said.

"Then why didn't you give me the heads-up about your nephew coming on board?"

"I couldn't. Rex and I were sworn to secrecy by Jocko. He didn't want competitors to preempt us on the announcement. Otherwise, I would have said something. I always got your back, Kingpin. You know that. Relax." He reached a greasy hand toward Whitherspoon, who stepped out of reach to avoid getting touched.

"Another thing. Did you contact the Picklers? Carl told me someone at the station said I got him fired."

Rump leaned against the bench and folded his arms. "Did he *say* I said something?"

"No, he wouldn't tell me who said it, but you're the only one who knows anything—besides me."

"Calm down. I didn't say a thing. He's guessing, trying to trick you into admitting something. Don't be so damn gullible. He knows nothing."

"If he knows nothing, why is he so pissed at me?" Whitherspoon said as sweat beaded on his forehead.

"'Cause you're the Kingpin and he's jealous!" Rump sighed. "You know the drill. You've been through it many times. Envy makes people do awful things."

—⚊—

The next day, while leaning back in his chair, feet crossed on top of the desk, Strollo was munching on a bag of Cheetos when his phone rang.

"Strollo."

"Detective Strollo?"

"Yes, who's this?"

"Samantha Ayres from Briggs News 20."

"Hello, Ms. Ayres. By the way, feel free to call me Louis."

"I contacted Corporate. Unless served a court order, we can't test the DNA of employees without their knowledge and permission. It's against company policy."

"OK. Thanks for checking. We can get a court order or collect their DNA through what we call a 'garbage pull,' by taking it from an abandoned personal article like a cigarette or drink can."

"OK."

"We have now confirmed what I suggested to you when we first met. There's a definite relationship between the killer of Manuel Dominguez and Briggs News 20."

"Sorry to hear that. Please keep me informed."

"Will do. I have a question, Ms. Ayres."

"Please...Samantha."

"Samantha, did any guests tour your TV station after hours on April first?"

"I'll check the calendar. Let me see...April first...I don't see anything. We didn't have an employee orientation or guest tour that day, I can tell you that. Sometimes Ad Sales brings clients in. Jocko does too. I'll check with them. Why do you ask?"

"I can answer that question better in person. Mind if I stop by?"

"When?"

"How 'bout now?" he asked.

"Give me half an hour to ask Jocko about it and to take care of a few things."

"I'll finish lunch and see you in thirty minutes." He ate the last of the Cheetos, squeezed the empty bag into a ball, and banked it off his desk into the wastebasket. He washed up and then loaded his briefcase.

—⁂—

Meanwhile, at Briggs Lake News, Samantha opened her purse, removed her compact, and examined herself in the small mirror. She touched her hair, patting both sides near her ears, applied plum lip gloss, and refreshed her bronze makeup. She smiled to check her teeth, making sure they had no trace of lip gloss. She finished her touch-up by dabbing a few drops of perfume on each side of her face before calling Jocko to ask if he or anyone from the advertising sales department had given a studio tour on April first.

Thirty minutes later, Strollo sat in her office at a table near the window. He opened his briefcase and removed a folder with his notes and sorted them. Then he took out an envelope, opened it, and removed copies of photographs, setting them on the table.

Samantha liked the shape of Strollo's muscular upper body and the way it formed a solid outline beneath his creased suit.

She admired the gentle way he sifted through the documents, organizing them for her inspection.

"Look familiar?" Strollo asked.

His question jolted her from her thoughts about Strollo's physical attributes. "Yes. We use them for investors and advertising clients. They're brochures and marketing pieces designed to promote the station."

Strollo returned the documents to his briefcase.

"These are copies of documents found in the backseat of the taxi of the murdered driver. The killer may have visited your station on April first, the night of the murder. That's why I asked you about who might have been at the TV station that night."

"That's terrible," Samantha said. "But why would the killer leave the brochures at the crime scene?"

"I don't know."

"He could've done it on purpose to throw you off."

"True. We'll find out as I track down all the clues."

Their eyes met.

"You look like something's on your mind," he said.

"When you first met me, you looked surprised that I was the director of human resources. Was that because I'm black?"

"No. Because you're beautiful."

She smiled, revealing teeth so perfect they could have been in a toothpaste commercial. "Thank you. That's very kind of you to say."

"It's the truth."

Her smile lit up her face. She looked down for a moment to collect her thoughts, took a deep breath, and then looked back at Strollo. "I checked with Jocko. He didn't give anyone a tour on April first, and neither did Ad Sales. The only other explanation is that someone else could have given a personal tour—after hours."

"Can you give me a list of all the station personnel who would have access to the building after normal operating hours?"

"I can do better than that. I can pull a report that shows who used their security card to get in the building on that date, when they entered, and when they left," she said.

"When?"

"Right now." She opened a file on her computer and within a few minutes had the appropriate security card report. "On the evening of April first, three employees entered the building after hours."

"Who?"

"Thomas Whitherspoon, Leon Rump...and Carl Pickler."

Strollo cleared his throat. "Can you set up a meeting with Whitherspoon and Rump so we can find out what they were doing that night?"

"Sure," Samantha said. "Just let me know when you want to do it."

"You have security cameras throughout the building. Can you access the video of the night of the murder?"

Samantha nodded. "I'll check with Leon, he's in charge of maintaining the security cameras."

"Thanks. There's one more thing. Early in my investigation, I asked if there were any racial conflicts among your employees. You said everything was fine."

"It *was* fine." Samantha tapped her long, polished fingernails on the table.

"Then why did I read in the paper a few days later that you were investigating Pickler for complaints of racism?" He looked into her eyes.

"I had to protect his confidentiality—company policy." She shrugged and looked out the window in the direction of the parking lot, where the sound of a car alarm gave her a welcome relief from the look he was giving her. "At the time, I didn't know the seriousness or validity of the concerns."

"Really? They were serious enough for Pickler to resign."

She looked back at Strollo, her smile gone. "What do you mean by that?"

"I'm investigating a homicide. When I ask questions, I expect truthful answers."

"OK, fine," Samantha said.

They stared at each other.

"Good," he said.

"Good. Anything else?"

"Not for now." He rose to his feet and nodded.

She bowed her head slightly in return, opened her office door, and held it as he passed through. Neither said good-bye. She remained in the doorway, still clutching her notepad and pen, studying him as he walked down the hallway. When he disappeared from view, she reentered her office and leaned toward the window so she could watch him get in his car and drive away. When he drove out of sight, she dropped her notepad and pen on the desk, picked up her cell phone. *I can't let him leave like this. I need to tell him I'm sorry. I care about this man.*

She punched in Strollo's number. Her call went to voice mail, so she hung up.

Strollo had received a call seconds earlier.

"Hey, Louie. Shayne. Forensic results arrived. The blood DNA is from Manuel Dominguez, and there is DNA from a second individual. Thought you'd want to know."

"Yes."

"The toxicology report indicates no drugs in the victim's body—confirms blunt-force trauma as cause of death."

"Thanks, Shayne. Get me a court order to take DNA samples from Briggs News 20 employees." When the call ended, he threw his cell phone on the front seat next to him and turned on his radio in time to hear one of his favorite Beatles love songs, and he was glad.

—◌—

The next day, Strollo drove to the crime scene and paced along the lake, looking for clues and thinking about the killer's motive. He rested on a park bench and watched the gulls racing along the shore. He smelled the fresh lake air and heard the wind rustling in the palm trees. *It's hard to imagine that a guy's life was brutally snuffed out in such a picturesque spot.*

A thought popped into his mind. *It's Saturday. Samantha Ayres is home. I'll pay her a visit and ask her to dinner. I might have been too harsh yesterday when I confronted her about not telling me of the accusations against Pickler. I could smooth things out over dinner.*

Strollo knew where she lived; detectives made it a habit of gathering useful information. He parked a few houses down from Samantha's. Her house, nestled in an upscale community, had the classic Spanish design of homes in the Southwest: a tile roof and stucco siding with a wall around the yard to protect against windstorms. High ceilings and large windows strategically placed on the property reflected sunlight and highlighted the architecture of the house. Various cacti and ornamental rock adorned the front yard. The irrigation system in the backyard promoted a bountiful grass lawn. Its grapefruit and orange trees, decorated with vivid colors, gave him a whiff of their tangy scent. *This lady's done all right. Her lawn looks as manicured as the fairways at Augusta.*

A car pulled into her driveway. Strollo ducked behind a palm tree. Samantha got out of the driver's side and a handsome young African American man emerged from the passenger's seat. They walked to her door, hand in hand, chatting and laughing. The young man opened the door for her and they entered her home. *So she's got a boyfriend!* Strollo, hands in his pockets, walked down the center of the street to his car. He turned the key to the ignition, and a sad song about loneliness blasted through his stereo speakers that described how he felt.

—⁂—

When Strollo arrived home, Hannah pounced. "Did you remember about Arizona State's coach coming to scout my next game?"

"Yes, but I don't think I can make it."

"Daddy, you promised!" Hannah's eyes pleaded as tears streamed down her cheeks.

"I said I would *try* to make it to your game, but it would depend on my work."

"My whole future's at stake here. How can you do this to me?" Hannah cried.

Strollo tried to put his arms around his daughter, but Hannah pushed him away.

"I love you and would do anything for you. You know that," he said.

"Do I? Then go to the game if you love me. My friends' dads go to every game. Some dad you are!"

"There's a killer out there somewhere in our community, and I've got to find him and stop him before he kills again."

"You're not the only guy who works for the police department, you know. Why does it always have to be you?"

"It's my job, sweetie."

"What about me? The coach wants to meet you. He's thinking of giving me a scholarship. Without a scholarship, I have no money for college."

"Your mama—I had to pay a lot of hospital bills. I did the best I could," Strollo said.

"Mama's illness is your excuse for everything. I'm tired of us never having enough money, and it sucks that you can't be there for me when I need you. Your work is more important than me—every time."

"That's not true." Strollo reached his hand out to his daughter. She left it stranded, turning around and marching out of the room, slamming the door behind her.

Strollo opened the refrigerator, found a beer on the bottom shelf, popped it open, stuffed a bag of potato chips under his arm, and headed for the basement followed by his old golden retriever, Kenzie.

He set his snacks on the end table next to his overstuffed recliner positioned in front of a flat-screen TV mounted on the wall. He sunk into the chair and turned on the TV.

Kenzie rested her head against his knee. He patted the golden retriever's head. "You're such a good dog."

Kenzie licked his hand.

Chapter 7

ANOTHER CHANCE

"Sure wish you'd give me advance notice before scheduling things like this, Jocko. I would've bought a new suit and had my hair done." Whitherspoon bounced his fingers on the desk. "My image has to be protected."

Jocko smiled. "You're in good hands. Stephanie's a hairstylist and makeup artist. She'll make you look good. I promise."

Whitherspoon looked serious. "If she doesn't, you've wasted your money."

"No worries, big guy," Jocko said.

"My brand's everything. You know that."

"Haven't I always guarded your brand with my life?" Jocko cocked his head and placed his hand on Whitherspoon's shoulder. "Cool it."

During the walk-through for a newscast, Jocko had entered the studio, leading Charles Buck and his assistant, Stephanie Angel. They were carrying black bags. After introducing them, Jocko explained to Whitherspoon and Martin that the photographers were hired to take photos of the coanchors for a marketing campaign.

Charles seemed fit for a man in his sixties, despite his thinning gray hair. He assembled light stands and turned on a tape of easy-listening music, which created a soothing atmosphere.

Stephanie's smile, even brighter than her blue eyes, continued nonstop as she set up her makeup chair.

"Who wants to go first?" Jocko asked.

"I will," Martin said.

"OK. Have fun, kids." Jocko waved and left the studio.

Stephanie motioned for Martin to sit in her chair and began combing his hair. "You need a little trim." Using her handheld mirror, she showed him a rebellious tuft of hair. "Mind if I clean it up a little bit?"

"Go right ahead," Martin said.

"It won't take long." She snipped and combed his hair, and then powdered his face. "You have a small scar on your forehead, so I put a little makeup on it. I hope you don't mind."

"Thanks, Miss Stephanie," Martin said as he switched chairs for his headshots. "Charles, you have your work cut out for you. I don't photograph well."

"It's easy taking a good picture of a handsome guy like you," Charles said as he cradled his camera's big lens in the palm of his left hand. He avoided the technique of counting "Three...two... one." He preferred to capture spontaneity rather than a pose.

Charles snapped pictures from all angles while Stephanie held the round, gold reflector, which projected light upward, creating a warmer skin tone. He knew his subjects would mirror his facial expressions without coaching and adopt his natural, relaxed poses. The photographer evoked the mood he wanted in the subject and then captured it time and time again on his camera.

"OK, we're done." Charles brought his viewfinder close to Martin so he could see the pictures. "What do you think?"

Martin watched while Charles advanced the pictures. "They look good. Choose the ones you like. You're the expert," Martin said.

Charles turned to the anchor desk. "We're ready for you, Mr. Whitherspoon. Stephanie will get you fixed up while I make some adjustments to the light stands."

Stephanie motioned for Whitherspoon to sit in her makeup chair. Then she put a cover around him and combed his hair.

"You trimmed Rex's hair. Aren't you going to do anything with mine?"

"I don't think so, Mr. Whitherspoon. Your hair looks fine."

"For your sake, I hope you're right. Did you hear what I said to Jocko?"

"About your brand? Yes, sir." Stephanie smiled. "I'll take good care of your brand."

"I need you to take good care of me," he said.

"I said I would, Mr. Whitherspoon."

"I mean exceptional care."

"I'm not sure I know what you're talking about."

Whitherspoon reached his hand from under the cover and groped her upper thigh.

Stephanie pushed his hand away, her face turning bright red. In a few minutes, she applied makeup, eyeliner and powder, and escorted Whitherspoon to the portrait chair, where Charles was making last-minute lighting adjustments.

Charles shot a batch of serious poses from all angles followed by smiling poses, employing the same technique used on Martin. When Charles finished, he showed them to Whitherspoon.

"I don't like any of these," Whitherspoon said. "Redo them. You make me look like an old fart!"

"Sorry, Mr. Whitherspoon. I'll delete these and we'll start over." Charles took several dozen more shots.

Then Charles held up the viewfinder to show Whitherspoon the second set of images.

Whitherspoon smiled. "OK, I like these a lot better, but you'll retouch them, right? I want all the wrinkles out or I won't give them my final OK. You got that?"

"No problem, Mr. Whitherspoon. You'll have a complexion as smooth as a baby's butt. I'll e-mail them tomorrow for your approval."

"All right," Whitherspoon said. "Now you're talking."

At the close of the session, Charles took a dozen shots of both anchors at the news desk. When given the chance to look at them, Whitherspoon frowned. "No good. I'm not happy. I'll show you where to shoot so my face gets the proper lighting."

With Whitherspoon setting up each shot, they stayed fifteen minutes longer until he felt satisfied he looked good in all of them. Charles and Stephanie packed their equipment and walked toward the studio exit.

Whitherspoon whispered a comment to Martin loud enough for Stephanie to hear and laughed at his own remark. Stephanie stopped and turned around. "What did you say?"

"Nice ass!"

Stephanie set her case down and marched to the anchor desk, where Whitherspoon and Martin were sitting. She slapped Whitherspoon so hard he rocked on two legs of the stool and had to grab the edge of the desktop with both hands to keep from falling off backward. Martin burst out laughing but caught himself, covered his mouth with one hand, and looked at the floor.

Whitherspoon glared at Stephanie, his hair as chaotic as his thoughts. The imprint of her right hand remained on the side of his face.

"How do you like *my* brand?" she said and stomped out.

Martin caught his breath, composed himself, put his hand on Whitherspoon's shoulder, and said, "Gee, Kingpin, some women just can't take a compliment."

—w—

A few days later, after the last newscast, a screeching siren disrupted the serenity of a clear summer evening. Jocko looked out his window in time to see EMTs wheeling Thomas Whitherspoon out of the building into a waiting ambulance. He ran downstairs and was assured by Carol that she would follow the ambulance to the hospital and give him a report later in the evening on Whitherspoon's condition.

Whitherspoon woke up looking at the ceiling and shut his eyes when a flash of light temporarily blinded him. *What's that smell?* Lying on his back, he turned his head and opened his eyes again to see tubes in both arms and heart monitor sensors attached to his chest. A man with glowing eyes and wearing the blue polo shirt of a hospital volunteer, had his hand on the bed rail and had positioned himself close to Whitherspoon's face.

"Where am I?"

"Intensive care unit," said the man in the blue shirt.

"What happened?"

"A heart attack. You'd be dead now if Carol Lackey hadn't called nine-one-one," the man said. "You were sitting at your cubicle, packing up to leave, and collapsed. She waited here until all the tests were done on you before going home for the night."

"What are you doing here?" Whitherspoon asked.

"I volunteered for this."

Whitherspoon tried to sit up, but a pain in his chest forced him back down, and he lay on his side. "Who are you anyway?"

"I'm the man kicked out of Hoochy's when you and Pickler were having lunch. I had to keep him from sharing something with you. You would have used it to hurt him."

"Oh yeah. You were yelling something about shut up, and they threw you out."

"Yes. Not very dignified, but it worked. My distraction gave Pickler enough time to reconsider telling you anything." He stepped closer and put his hand on the railing of the bed.

Whitherspoon studied his visitor. "Were you the guy I gave twenty bucks to outside of the studio?"

"Yes, and the guy you threatened to call the police on," he said.

"Man, you sure get around," Whitherspoon said. "What's your name?"

"My name's Eli."

Eli, where have I heard that name? "Aren't you the guy who witnessed the Lakeside murder? Strollo's looking for you, you know. You're a person of interest."

"Strollo doesn't need any more help from me. He'll solve it."

"Instead of just watching, why didn't you do something to help Manny Dominguez while he was getting pummeled to death?"

"What could I have done? Those men each made choices. It wasn't my place to interfere with their free will."

Whitherspoon extended his hand and grabbed Eli's arm. "What are you doing here?"

"After your last episode with death, you promised to change your ways. Why didn't you?"

His words pierced Whitherspoon like needles. "I tried to help the Picklers. They didn't want my help. I tried to reconcile with my ex-wife, Naomi. She remarried. What'd you expect me to do?"

"Don't give up. Keep looking for ways to help others."

"What about my 'Good News Show'? That's helping others."

"What do you mean?"

"I've gotten a lot of publicity from it, and it's increased my stature in the community."

"Yeah, it's all about you, isn't it? You're only using the show to promote yourself. You're doing it for recognition. Doing good works should be its own reward."

Whitherspoon broke down and cried so hard he had trouble catching his breath. He put his hands over his face. "I'm so sorry. I want another chance to make things right. I don't want to die!"

Eli patted Whitherspoon on the shoulder. "You know right from wrong. Do the right thing no matter what it costs."

"Am I going to die?" Whitherspoon asked.

"Not today."

About an hour later a nurse came to check on Whitherspoon. She recorded the readings from the heart monitor to her hand-held computer. "Are you awake, Mr. Whitherspoon?"

"Yes."

"How are you feeling?"

"I feel pretty good."

"Your blood pressure and heart rate have changed since my last visit an hour ago. Now they're in the normal range. It's nothing short of a miracle. Wait until your doctor sees this." She couldn't stop smiling as she tucked his bed sheets and moved Whitherspoon's water glass closer on the nightstand. "You're on the mend."

—⚏—

The next morning after he was served breakfast, Whitherspoon had a visitor.

"Jocko, so nice of you to come."

"Hi Tom, I couldn't leave the Kingpin in a hospital room and not check on him. The nurses tell me you've had quite a miraculous turnaround."

"Yeah. They thought at first I had a heart attack, but now they're not so sure. I actually feel pretty good. The docs want to run some tests and then I should get released in a day or two."

Jocko smiled. "That's good to hear, my friend." Looking up, he pointed at the TV mounted on the wall. "I'll bet it's tuned to Briggs News 20."

"Absolutely."

—⚏—

"Welcome to Briggs News 20. This is Rex Martin. Thomas Whitherspoon has the night off." Martin proceeded to anchor the Friday newscast. After reading the news, he tossed to Ronnie for sports and Erin for weather before closing out the show.

No other mention was made of Whitherspoon's trip to the hospital the night before. Jocko watched the newscast from the studio and made several suggestions during the commercial breaks. After sign-off, he invited Martin into his office. "Nicely done, Rex. You're catching on quick."

"Thanks, Mr. Moore."

"I'm assigning you to cover the homicide investigation. Kingpin wanted to do a series on the Lakeside murder, but he hasn't done much with it. He's been wrapped up in his 'Good News Show,' and now he's in the hospital for a few days."

"I heard from Carol he had a coronary."

"They thought that at first, but when I visited him this morning they weren't so sure and are going to run some more tests."

"I'll get right on it," Martin said. "I've got a lot of experience with hard news and crime investigations, especially serial killers."

"I know." Jocko nodded. "I remember."

"Kingpin obviously has some medical concerns to deal with, and his age may be an issue too," Martin said. "You can count on me. I have his back."

"Thanks."

—⁂—

On Monday morning Samantha stuck her head in Jocko's doorway. "Hey, boss. Got a few minutes?"

"Sure. Come on in. I need to talk to you, too. What's going on?"

"I want to bring you up to speed on a few things. First of all, I spoke with Whitherspoon this morning, and he says he's fine and will be coming back to work in the next day or so."

"I know, I talked to him myself. He sounds good. What else?"

"Do you recall me asking if you had given anyone an after-hours tour of the office on the night of the Lakeside murder?"

"Yeah. Neither Ad Sales nor I had given an after-hours tour." Jocko pointed to a chair at his conference table. "Go ahead. Sit down."

"Thanks." She sat down and crossed her legs. "Detective Strollo asked me to check the security card reader report from that day to see if anyone else returned to the office after we closed and to retrieve video from our security cameras."

"And what'd you come up with?"

"The security video cams were disabled that day. The card reader report had three names: Tom Whitherspoon, Carl Pickler, and Leon Rump."

"Jeez. You don't think those guys could kill someone in cold blood do you?" Jocko rubbed the top of his bald head from back to front and back again.

"I don't know, but Briggs News 20 brochures were found in the taxi, so there may be a link to our station."

"Now what do we do?"

"Strollo's getting a court order to take DNA and fingerprint samples from Whitherspoon and Rump. According to company policy, we'll have to cooperate." She exhaled and glanced at the row of Emmy statues on Jocko's credenza. "We're going to interview them in my office and find out what they were doing in the office after hours on April first, which was the night of the murder."

Jocko went to the window, hands clasped behind his back. "What do we tell them?"

"Nothing. Strollo doesn't want them to know they're under suspicion; they might lawyer up and make it harder for him to get information."

Jocko shook his head. "I'll be honest. I don't like this business one bit. Two of my top employees are murder suspects and Strollo's asking us to take samples from them like they're common criminals. It's not right."

"DNA sampling could be a good thing—prove them innocent—exonerate them as suspects."

"OK. Then how're we going to get DNA and fingerprints without their knowledge?"

"We'll hire Charles Buck to take some promotional photos. His assistant, Stephanie, will get hair samples when she does their hair and makeup for the shoot. They work with the police from time to time as subcontractors. Strollo says it's legal and the evidence can be used in court."

Jocko laughed.

"What?" she asked.

"Trying to picture Leon and Kingpin allowing someone to cut their precious hair. They'll have a hissy fit." Jocko smiled. "Leon's a good engineer, but heaven help you if you mess with his ponytail."

Samantha pursed her lips and tightened the grip on her pen. "I'll tell her to leave the ponytail alone."

"Won't they be suspicious? They just had a photo shoot." Jocko said.

"We'll tell them this is a photo shoot for a special marketing campaign, and we'll include Leon Rump, Erin, and Ronnie Gaboni besides shooting Whitherspoon and Martin."

"What's Strollo doing about Pickler since he doesn't work here anymore?"

"Strollo will set up a meeting with Pickler at the police station and get his DNA at that time."

Still staring out his window, Jocko rested his hands on the windowsill. "I hate to even think this, but Pickler, who seems like such a nice guy, may not only be a racist—he could be a killer too."

Samantha looked down.

Jocko spun away from the window and faced Samantha. His hands fell to his sides. "Anything else?"

"That's it. You had something for me, sir?" She leaned toward him.

"Yeah. I know the timing couldn't be worse, but I think for the good of the station, it's time to let him go."

"Who?"

"Whitherspoon."

"What!" She dropped her pen on the floor.

"His salary's too high for what we're getting out of him. On the nights he's off, there's little difference in the ratings. It has nothing to do with his health issues. Personally, I like Tom, always have. But this is business. "

Samantha stared at Jocko. "It's going to look to Whitherspoon and others like you're doing it because of his health."

"We talked about doing this last year, remember?"

"Last year we were talking about replacing him with Pickler—he's gone. Who'll take Whitherspoon's place?"

"Rex."

"Rex? Do you really think that's a good idea?"

"He's doing real well, and the crew likes him."

"That may be true, but he hasn't proven himself. He's anchored the news for only a few weeks."

"I know." Jocko nodded. "But I have a gut feeling about this. Besides, we won't do it right away. We'll do it over a period of months."

Samantha bit her lower lip. "That's what we tried to do with Carl. You began grooming Carl for advancement, Whitherspoon didn't like it one bit—he felt so threatened—didn't seem to help him at all. And in fact, when Pick had to resign, Whitherspoon actually seemed happy about it. Didn't you tell me he asked if he could anchor the news solo on a permanent basis?"

"Yeah. You're right."

"Why would his reaction change this time around?"

"Trust. Whitherspoon trusts Rex. He never trusted Pick."

"I don't know about that. I think Whitherspoon will sue us."

"For what?"

"Age discrimination. He won't go quietly, or cheaply for that matter."

"Lawsuits are very expensive. You're right—he would sue. Not that he needs the money," Jocko said.

"What do you mean, he doesn't need the money?"

"Kingpin's loaded. He's rich. He didn't start out that way, though—worked his way through college and supported himself when he got his first gig as a reporter in Cody."

Samantha picked her pen up from the carpet. "Don't tell me he got rich working as a reporter in Cody, Wyoming."

"No, he didn't. His folks sold land in Wyoming to the Arco Richfield Group. They discovered vast coal deposits and developed them into what became known as the Black Thunder Coal Mine, the largest single coal mine operation in the world. His parents were smart enough to keep the mineral rights to the land—very shrewd decision. They got paid a fee for every ton of coal mined. Whitherspoon inherited a bundle when they passed. His older brother drowned in a swimming accident, making him their sole heir."

"I don't get it. Why's he so concerned with being the Kingpin if he doesn't need the money?"

"It's not about the money. For Whitherspoon, anchoring news on live, prime-time TV is like smack is to a junkie. He needs the nightly ego fix. It's everything to him." Jocko sighed and sat down at his desk, folding his hands in front of him.

"If that's the case, what's he doing in a midsized Arizona city instead of New York?"

"He could have gone to New York, but he likes the West. The guy would rather be a big fish in a little pond than a little fish in a big pond," Jocko explained.

"This shark's going to have to find a different place to swim." Samantha took a breath, lost in thought.

"Exactly." Jocko leaned back in his chair with his hands behind his head. "I have a strategy figured out, but I'd like your thoughts on how to avoid expensive litigation."

She replied, "We restructure News. We give him sixty days advanced notice, or pay in lieu of notice, plus anything due from his contract. We could eliminate positions of younger workers as part of the reorganization of the news department, which creates a firewall protecting us from an age discrimination suit."

"Terminate a bunch of young people for the sole purpose of covering our ass?" Jocko frowned.

"That's not what I meant. If we restructure departments and eliminate positions to stay competitive in the marketplace and those changes happen to include younger employees, we'll be OK. In that scenario, Whitherspoon couldn't claim age discrimination."

"Is there another way?"

"When his contract runs out, don't renew it. Tell him we're taking news in a different direction. That's my recommendation as long as you can wait until his contract expires."

"Six months. I can handle that. I'll phase him out of high-profile news reporting—like local crime—give more to Rex." Jocko rested his chin on his right hand.

"Like we did with Pick last year," Samantha said. "Again, I have to ask, what makes you think it would be different this time around with Rex."

"OK. Here's my plan. We talk to Whitherspoon ahead of time."

Samantha lowered her voice to imitate Jocko. "'Hey, Kingpin, what's happening? Oh, by the way, we're terminating you. Have a nice day.'"

"Not like that." Jocko smiled. "We'll give him an incentive to cooperate."

"What kind of incentive?"

"We'll offer a six-month victory lap climaxed with a sixty-minute special filled with his best clips—on-air highlights. He'll eat it up. We'll sell it to him as his grand send-off."

"And if he doesn't go for the idea, then what? We know he's not ready to retire, and he's not in it for the money either." Samantha gazed at Jocko.

"I have an ace in the hole. Rex witnessed Whitherspoon sexually harassing Stephanie, the photographer's assistant. With that kind of leverage, I think we can get Whitherspoon to cooperate."

"Rex never said anything to me about it. Neither did *she* for that matter."

"He saw it all in the studio one day and came and reported it to me. Felt I should know what Whitherspoon had done."

"What'd he do?"

"He told her she had a nice ass."

Samantha shook her head. "What'd she do when he said that?"

"She slapped him. Rex thinks he can get her to file a formal complaint, too, and he'd verify as a witness."

"He'd go on the record against Whitherspoon?"

"Absolutely. We've already discussed it. He told me he'd do it if I wanted."

Samantha arched her eyebrows. "So much for loyalty."

"When it comes to their careers, talent are ruthless. You know that—a bunch of piranhas."

"Whitherspoon could still get a lawyer and fight the charges or just quit," she said.

"Sure. But he'd look bad. He hates looking bad. And, he'd surrender the remaining value of his contract, his nightly ego fix, and his send-off special. He's not going anywhere."

"I had no idea you were up to all this." A smile tugged at her face.

"That's why *I* get paid the big bucks, Samantha." He winked.

She rose from her chair. "Anything else?"

"No. Tell Strollo I'm on board and keep me posted."

Chapter 8

CHICKEN NOODLE SOUP

"Louis? This is Samantha. I'm calling to let you know I met with Jocko and we discussed getting the DNA samples and interviewing Rump and Whitherspoon. He wanted you to know he's on board with our plan."

"Oh, that's great, thanks," Strollo said.

"But a couple of problems. Whitherspoon's in the hospital for a few days. We can't interview him until he gets back to work."

"What happened?"

"At first they thought his heart stopped. Now they're not sure what happened. They're still doing tests, but he appears to be OK. The other problem is that for some reason the security cameras were turned off that night according to Rump."

"I'd like to meet with you, today if possible." he said.

"That's fine."

At that moment, the dispatcher interrupted their conversation with an urgent message on his two-way radio. "Detective Strollo, there's been another homicide on Lakeside Drive. Shayne Mendoza's on the scene and asked you to join him as soon as you can."

"Ten-four. I'll be right there."

Returning to his cell phone, he said, "Samantha, an emergency has come up, and I need to go to a crime scene. When I'm finished, I'll come to your office."

"I'll be here all day."

—⚅—

Strollo surveyed the crime scene with his assistant, Shayne Mendoza. He bent down to get a closer look at the splatters of blood around the restroom door. The similarities in the two Lakeside homicides struck him. "It looks like the same killer— both victims were Mexican cab drivers stabbed then hit over the head, but not robbed."

"Yeah. Very similar," Mendoza agreed.

"Shayne, what can you tell me about Mr. Escobar?" Strollo asked.

Holding his notepad in his left hand, Mendoza rattled off the contents of his scribbled notes. "Escobar was a legal Mexican immigrant with a good reputation in the community, known for working hard and sending money home to his parents in Mexico— had no wife—five-year-old son lived with his parents. Although stabbed numerous times, cause of death appears to be blunt-force trauma like the first Lakeside murder."

"Did the medical examiner finish the DNA sampling?" Strollo asked.

"Yes. We've dusted the area for fingerprints too and will run them through the National Crime Information Center in Washington, DC," Mendoza said.

"Any witnesses?"

"None."

"Alert all taxi and shuttle services to take extra precautions when accepting fares after ten o'clock," Strollo said.

"I'm on it."

"Good. Catch you later, Shayne." Strollo headed toward his car until he saw a pen glistening in the sun a few feet away. He detoured to pick it up. Holding it to the light, he read the inscription: "Briggs News 20, News Department."

—⚅—

Samantha's administrative assistant appeared in the doorway of her office. "The receptionist just called. Detective Louis Strollo's here to see you. He's sitting in the lobby."

"Thanks, Sheila Jean. Tell him it'll be a couple of minutes."

Oh no! He's here. I thought he'd call first. Samantha opened her compact, checked her hair, and touched up her lip gloss. *I guess that'll have to do.* She straightened the jacket and skirt of her business suit, brushing away the wrinkles and a speck of lint, before walking toward the lobby.

She saw Strollo sitting in a corner checking messages on his smartphone. "Hi, Louis. How are you?" She extended her hand.

He got up, put his phone in his pocket, and shook her hand. "Doing well, Samantha. How 'bout you?"

"Good. Thanks for asking," she said. *His hand is so warm.*

"Sorry I didn't call first. When we talked earlier you said you'd be here all day, so I thought I'd just come on over," Strollo explained.

"That's fine. Let's go to my office."

She led him down the hallway to the human resources department. Samantha possessed many abilities, one of which was a talent for walking in a way that would rivet a man's attention. She treated him to a demonstration and felt his appreciation all the way to her office. After pulling out a chair for Strollo at her small conference room table, she sat down opposite him.

"When we talked on the phone this morning, you were interrupted. What came up?"

"We have another slaughtered cab driver."

"Oh no!" Samantha shut her eyes. "That's terrible."

"Name's Chico Escobar. Does his name ring a bell? Any association with your TV station?"

Her expression said no. "Never heard of him. He doesn't have anything to do with our station as far as I know."

"OK. Thought I'd check. Now, let's talk about the best way to interview the guys who came into the studio on April first. I'll interview Pickler at the police station, get his DNA and finger-prints. What about Rump and Whitherspoon?"

"Probably the best way is for us to talk to them in my office on the same day."

"Pick a day that's good for you."

She leafed through her calendar and suggested three dates in the coming week.

"The first date works best for me," he said. "When we talk to Rump I'll ask him why there's no security video available for the night in question."

"Sounds good," she said as she marked the date on her calendar.

He entered it into his smartphone, hesitated for a moment, and then got up to leave.

Samantha rose from her chair, heart pounding. *Don't leave yet. Ask me something else. I've got all day. Come on, Samantha, tell him!* "Louis, there's something I have to tell you. I'm sorry about the way I reacted the last time you were here. I should have told you about the accusations against Pickler and my investigation. I really respect you—the last thing I would want is for you...for you...not to feel you can trust me." *There, I said it.*

Strollo considered the exquisite woman in front of him and smiled. "You were doing your job, and I was doing mine. Let's move on."

Samantha came around the table and hugged him. "Thanks, Louis."

The gesture surprised Strollo, whose arms remained frozen at his sides. When she released her grip, he smiled and with a nod left her office.

—⁂—

The next day, Strollo arrived early at the police station. He had a lot of work to do and made good progress until Rex Martin showed up unannounced.

"Thanks for seeing me without an appointment, Detective. I'm Rex Martin and I'm taking over the news coverage of local crime from Tom Whitherspoon. We'll be working together." Martin offered his hand and they shook.

"I heard you had replaced Carl Pickler on Briggs News 20. How do you like it so far?"

"I love it. Everyone has been so welcoming," Martin replied. "One of our producers spoke with your office earlier about the second Lakeside murder. What can you tell me about it?"

"Not much. We're still at the early stages of the investigation. We only discovered it yesterday."

"Do you think Briggs Lake has a serial killer on the loose?" Martin asked.

"I don't have any breaking news to share. Sorry." Strollo massaged his forehead with his fingertips. "We're still following up on leads."

"Are the Briggs News viewers using the police tip line?"

"It's hard to say." Strollo laughed. "They don't identify themselves as 'Briggs News Viewers.' After all, it's an *anonymous* tip line."

Martin grinned. "I guess you're right. Speaking of tips, I got a tip that Briggs News 20 brochures were found at the scene of the first Lakeside murder. Care to comment on that?" Martin said.

"No comment on that." Strollo's smile dissolved into thin air. *Where did he get that information? Except for my team, the only person I told was Samantha Ayres!*

"Didn't mean to set you off," Martin said.

"I'm not mad. It's just that I don't have anything to give you right now. I'll let you know when we develop anything newsworthy."

"Thanks, Detective." Martin waved. "I'll be in touch. Try to give me something for tonight's newscast."

—◆—

After Martin left police headquarters, Strollo called Samantha. "Could we get together? There are some things related to the murder investigations I need to discuss."

"Sure, Louis, but I'm stepping out for a bite to eat right now."

"Can I buy?"

"Sure."

"Where?"

"Hoochy's."

"Perfect. I'll meet you there, Samantha."

Hoochy's Bar and Grill rocked with the lunch crowd. The wait staff crisscrossed in full swing, carrying trays of drinks and food orders. The hostess escorted Samantha and Strollo to a corner booth through the efficient cacophony amid smells of coffee and french fries. He slouched as much as she strode tall and straight. She wore a royal blue business suit with a black belt and matching stockings. He wore his crumpled gray suit, loosened tie, and a big smile, which made his mustache seem to twitch in time to his steps. Two very different worlds colliding in full view compelled the attention of the other patrons. Every head turned and stared as they strolled through the dining room. Sparks seemed to discharge from their feet with every step.

"Your server's Trixie-Lee," the hostess said as she handed them menus.

Trixie-Lee sprang to the table, her long braid bouncing behind her like a tail. When she recognized her newest customers, a big smile swept across her face. "Two of my favorites—together."

"Yeah, Samantha's doing her good deed for the day: keeping a lonely old cop company as he takes nourishment."

"I can see that." Trixie smiled and looked at Samantha. "It's great to see the way you reach out to help the less fortunate."

Samantha nodded. "I do what I can."

"I'll say this for you, Detective. You can't go wrong taking a lady to lunch," Trixie said.

"That's right. And she's not just any lady—she's a very pretty lady." Strollo smiled and looked at Samantha.

Samantha smiled. "Thank you, Louis. You're not just any cop either." She opened her napkin and placed it on her lap in a way that would make Emily Post proud.

Strollo scanned his menu then looked up at Trixie-Lee. "Are you and Dirk going to Bike Week in Sturgis this year? It's in August, isn't it?"

"Yeah, it is. But we can't make it this year. He has to work. We'll go next year. Can I get you something to drink while you look over your menus?"

"Water for me," Samantha said.

"Iced tea, unsweetened, thanks." Strollo examined the menu as if it was a racing form. "I can never make up my mind. It all looks good—especially when I'm hungry."

Samantha nodded. "I know what you mean, but I'm going with the chef's salad. Say, I saw an article in the sports page about your daughter, Hannah. She must be quite the athlete."

"Yeah. Arizona State wants her to pitch for their women's softball team."

"You must be so proud." Samantha closed her menu and laid it on the table.

Strollo followed suit. "Yeah, I couldn't be prouder. Hey, you look so different outside of the station, so relaxed and natural."

"Thanks, I'll take that as a compliment."

"That's how it's meant. I noticed that you look really nice today—I guess that's all I'm trying to say."

"Thanks."

Strollo felt the blood rush to his face.

Trixie-Lee returned with their drinks. "What can I get you folks?"

"Samantha will have the chef's salad, and I'll have the grilled chicken sandwich with fries."

"What kind of salad dressing?" Trixie-Lee said to Samantha.

"Vinegar and oil on the side."

Trixie scurried to the kitchen with their orders.

"How's everything going at the station?" Strollo asked.

"Fine. There's the usual murmuring about Mr. Whitherspoon. The crew finds him difficult to work with. They prefer working with Rex Martin."

Strollo straightened his chair. "Samantha, that's what I wanted to talk to you about. Mr. Martin came in to see me today. He's reporting on my investigations, and I'm sharing some information with him as I did with Whitherspoon."

"Yes. Whitherspoon's had a recent medical problem, I can't get into the details due to privacy issues. We're lightening his load, giving more work to Rex Martin."

"Can I ask you some questions?"

"Go ahead." Samantha reverted to human resources director, her professional mode: the listening skills of a best friend, the accuracy of a CPA, and the questioning skills of a prosecutor.

"Martin asked about the Briggs News 20 brochures found at the Dominguez crime scene."

"Yes?" Her eyebrows moved and her hands tensed on the table in front of her.

Strollo looked around the room before continuing. "You're the only one I told about the brochures. I didn't tell anyone outside the police department and the DA's office. He said he got a tip. Did you say anything to Martin about the brochures?"

"Nothing. The only person I told was Jocko. He needs to know everything you tell me regarding Briggs News 20. He's in charge."

"I understand. Anyone else?"

"Nope."

"Would Jocko share that information with Martin?"

"I doubt it. Jocko's a lockbox. When he decides to hold information, dynamite couldn't get it out."

"OK. Thought I'd ask."

She felt his cold stare. "Do you still trust me, Louis?"

"Yep. You trust me?"

"Yes." She glanced around the dining room and lowered her voice. "As you suggested, I arranged for Charles Buck and his assistant, Stephanie, to return to the studio for a photo shoot so they can get DNA samples. They're standing by until Whitherspoon returns to work."

"Does Jocko know the photographers work for the police department on the side as subcontractors?"

"Yes. I told him."

She continued to look at Strollo and he continued to look at her. They stared at each other in silence until Trixie-Lee brought their food.

When Trixie-Lee returned to the kitchen, a smile exploded on her face.

—⚹—

After lunch with Samantha, Strollo drove to his office while going over their conversation in his mind. *She didn't say anything about the brochures to anyone except Jocko, and he can keep secrets. So how did Martin know we found station brochures at the Dominguez crime scene? Maybe Jocko isn't as closemouthed as she thinks he is. I hope she's telling the truth and isn't talking to someone else about my investigation. She sure is attractive. Wish she didn't have a boyfriend. I wonder how serious they are.*

He checked himself out in the rearview mirror. His hair looked tousled so he took one hand off the wheel to smooth it out. *I wonder what she thinks of me. I know she respects me as a detective in the same way I respect her as an HR director. Could there be more to it? I do think she likes me. Possibly she's only extending professional courtesy and I'm reading too much into it—wishful thinking. It doesn't matter anyway. Samantha's got a boyfriend. Too bad.*

—⚹—

That evening, Hannah Strollo and a bunch of her teammates gathered at a friend's house for a slumber party, so her dad took the opportunity to work late. The detective's time had been chewed up that day by the meetings with Martin and Samantha, so he planned to work late into the night to get caught up on paperwork. The chief of police had asked him for a summary of his investigations to placate the mayor, who had been placing increased pressure on the department for an arrest. The citizens of Briggs Lake, concerned that their safety and security had been breached, demanded arrests in the homicide cases or else a shakeup of the police department.

Strollo turned on his radio to help him think more clearly. Elvis Presley's voice filled his office and set the mood. Strollo listened to the entire song, frozen in thought. *Yeah, Elvis, I am lonely tonight.*

OK. Gotta get to work. I've got two dead cab drivers. Both were Mexicans, knifed and bludgeoned to death on Lakeside drive. We got fingerprints and DNA samples at each crime scene. Briggs News 20 brochures were found at the first crime scene. There were three employees from Briggs News 20 working late that night. I found a pen from Briggs News 20 at the second crime scene. There's got to be some connection. Maybe Pickler isn't all he claims to be. After all, someone at the station did accuse him of racism. There might be something to it. The nice-guy thing could be a big act.

His cell phone rang.

"Strollo."

"Louis, this is Samantha. Do you have a few minutes?"

"Sure. Give me a second." He turned off the radio and left Johnny Cash in Folsom Prison. "Go ahead."

"I hope it's not too late to call."

"Not at all. I'm working late, writing some reports for the chief. What can I do for you?"

"Still at the office? You're quite the workaholic."

"What's on your mind?"

"First of all, thanks for buying lunch today. I appreciated it very much. This is going to sound stupid, but I can't stop thinking about something."

"What?" Strollo tapped his pen on the desk.

"When we were in my office and I apologized. You said let's move on, and I hugged you. You just stood there with your arms at your sides. Did I offend you? If so, I'm really sorry."

Strollo sighed. "No. You didn't offend me at all. I just didn't think it would be right for me to show any affection since our relationship is professional and you're already in a personal relationship."

"Who in the world told you that?"

"Isn't there a handsome man in your life?"

"Where did you get that idea?"

"Well, isn't there a young man in your life? Be honest."

"The only man in my life right now is my son. He's in college and visited last weekend."

"Your son! Oh, I thought he was your boyfriend." Strollo tried not to let his relief show in his voice.

"How'd you see my son? Are you stalking me?"

Strollo heard the smile at the other end. "No. My work led me to your area on Saturday, so I thought I'd stop by and invite you to dinner. A few minutes after I arrived in your neighborhood, you drove up with this guy, and I thought—"

"You thought wrong. I'm about to heat up some soup. Why don't you join me for a late-evening snack?"

"Although I did have a luscious Cheetos dinner a while ago, I could probably make room for a little soup. What kind? I'm very picky."

"Chicken noodle."

"As a matter of fact, you're in luck. Chicken noodle happens to be my favorite."

"Good. This must be my lucky day."

"No. It's my lucky day," he said.

"Good thing you know where I live." She laughed.

Strollo laughed and the smile stayed on his face. "Yeah, good thing I had the foresight to do a little advanced research. My investigative skills are top-notch, you know."

"So I've heard," she said.

"I'll change clothes and come right over."

"Good. I'll keep it warm."

"You're talking about the soup, right?" Strollo asked.

"What's that supposed to mean?" Samantha purred.

"Whatever you want it to mean. I'll be right over."

After parking his car, Strollo paused in her driveway, surveying the home. He observed every detail and catalogued in his mind things most observers would fail to notice. *I'd hate to see her landscaping bill; she must pay a fortune to keep this place up.* He opened his car door and retrieved the bouquet of flowers he'd picked up from the food mart. *I hope she's not allergic to flowers. I should have asked. What if she is? I'm screwed.*

His hands trembled as he walked toward her front door. He paused to look over his shoulder at his car, a good habit he had gotten into early in his law enforcement career. Seeing it was all clear around the car, he sprang up the steps, two at a time, and rang the doorbell.

Samantha swung open the large wooden door. The candelabra behind her created a glowing silhouette around her lustrous, sleek figure. "Hi, Louis, thanks for stopping over. Samantha's diner is open for business."

"Here are some flowers I picked along the way. They were on the side of the road, and I couldn't resist." He extended his arm and placed them below her nose for inspection.

Taking them in her left hand, she closed the door. "They're gorgeous, Louis. Thank you so much." She smelled them with great ceremony and gave him a quick embrace, getting a whiff of the body wash from his recent shower.

"You're not allergic to flowers or anything are you?"

"Nope." She turned her back on him.

"What's the matter?"

She twirled around to face him, eyes glistening. "I'm fine. It's just that it's been a long time since anyone gave me flowers. They smell so good. Let's go into the kitchen so I can put them in a vase while you consume my delicious chicken noodle soup."

The kitchen had subdued lighting, and several scented candles were burning. The room's dominant colors were black and red, which reminded Strollo of a steak house he frequented. The large tiles on the floor were charcoal gray. The skylight in the ceiling allowed him to see the stars shining in the clear evening sky. He thought the kitchen would be well lit in the daytime thanks to those skylights. He smelled the glorious aroma of fresh, hot chicken noodle soup and his mouth watered.

Strollo flopped into a seat in front of the large bowl of soup. Steam rose from it. Samantha bent over the sink filling the vase with water, enabling Strollo to study her slim figure wrapped in loose-fitting black slacks and a red blouse. *I wonder if she picked the combination of black slacks and a red blouse to match her kitchen. Probably. She's got it together.*

He looked down and noticed a stain he missed when he chose this pair of jeans. *I thought these were clean. Maybe she won't notice. She will. She notices everything. I wonder if she's thinking she's out of my league. She did invite me over after all, so she must have some interest. You're reading too much into this, Louie. Calm down.*

Turning around, vase in hand, her expression serious, "Aren't you going to eat?"

"Yes. Waiting for it to cool a little." At her prompt, he let a little soup overflow into the spoon and lifted it to his mouth, smelled the delicious aroma, and then tilted the spoon and its golden contents into his mouth. He felt the warm liquid go down his throat, chest, and stomach in slow motion. "This is the best-tasting chicken noodle soup I've ever had."

"I'll bet you say that to all the girls. I'm glad my soup meets with your approval. I'm pretty good at opening cans and heating their contents."

"I'll say. You're a master."

She smiled that killer smile, and placed the flowers on her kitchen counter.

Strollo pointed his spoon at the flowers. "Those flowers look like they were born to be on this counter."

Samantha's facial expression showed her agreement. "Would you like a glass of wine?" she asked.

"Sure."

"Red or white?"

"Doesn't matter. You pick something out."

"Then I'll open a bottle of sauvignon blanc. It goes well with the chicken soup."

Strollo observed the way she removed the cork and poured two large glasses while he finished the soup. *Don't spill, Strollo. You don't want the lady to think you're a slob.*

She set his glass of wine on the table in front of him. "If you're done, I'll show you around."

"All done." He got up and held his glass of wine toward her. "Thank you for the delicious dinner."

They touched glasses and looked into each other's eyes over the top of their glasses before sipping their wine.

Samantha led the way as both carried their wineglasses. "C'mon. First is my office, slash den, slash library, slash project room." She led him to a room with a large desk and a curtain shut behind a large picture window. A bookshelf lined one wall and a trophy case the other.

"Everyone should have a room like this." Strollo stopped at the trophy case and examined the statues and figurines. "What are all these for?"

"News awards mostly. I received some local Emmys a few years back as the senior news anchor."

"You were in news?"

"I guess you could say I used to be the Kingpin."

"I'm impressed, but I don't remember you being a newscaster."

"Do you remember Sammy Pearl? The short Afro?"

"You're Sammy Pearl? I can't believe it."

"One in the same. Pearl was my married name."

"Why'd you quit?"

"I didn't. Jocko reinvented me. He needed a local human resources director and thought I would be a good choice."

"Why you?"

"I got old. Jocko wanted a fresh young face to read the news, to attract youthful viewers, so at age thirty, I transitioned into human resources."

"Whitherspoon's a fresh young face? You've got to be kidding me." He laughed out loud at the thought.

"He's fifteen years older than me, except Whitherspoon's a guy and they get more of a pass when they age. Their on-air careers usually last longer than women's, with a few exceptions. Actually, it wasn't Whitherspoon who replaced me."

"Who did?"

"A pretty young thing who apparently looked perkier than me but was dumber than a cactus and just as prickly. Whitherspoon got hired a few years later after Jocko finally gave up on Miss Perky."

"It's not fair."

"I was OK with going off the air. Human resources is a more stable career than television news, and as a single mom, I could work days and be home for dinner with Chip."

Looking at a display of crowns and engraved cups, Strollo asked, "What're these for?"

"Beauty pageants. The scholarship money I made competing paid my college tuition. I used to be Miss Arizona—the first black Miss Arizona in fact—and I made it to the top ten at Miss America."

"Wow. You've sure kept that a well-guarded secret."

"In the news business, being a beauty queen can be a drawback. People tend to stereotype you as just another lightweight with a pretty face. Journalism credibility is more on how you write and speak than how you look."

"But this is TV. You're in front of the camera. You need to be beautiful."

"No. You have to be likeable, attractive, and have a pleasing voice. A beautiful woman has to work twice as hard to earn respect, and being black made it even tougher."

"It's a crazy world. Working in TV news is harder if you're beautiful." Strollo looked down. "Who knew?"

"It's true. People's first impression is that you were hired only for your looks."

"Unbelievable," he said.

"Good thing I'm not a blond." She laughed then took a sip of her wine. "Enough of this. Let's sit in my living room."

They strolled into her living room, decorated with taste and style. Strollo paused in front of two large windows, which gave a spectacular view of the property. A fifty-four-inch flat-screen, high-definition TV caught Strollo's eye. It was mounted on an inner wall, positioned so the screen could be seen with ease from any of the large leather chairs or couch.

After they sat down next to each other on a burgundy couch, Samantha turned to face Strollo. "We've talked enough about me. Your turn."

"I lost my wife to cancer years ago. Although she battled bravely, in the end she lost the fight. Cancer sucks. Hannah and my work were the only things that kept me going. I wanted to make sure Hannah had everything I could give her."

"From what I've seen and heard about Hannah, you've done that."

"Thanks, but I never feel like I've done enough. I've got high standards—so does Hannah, unfortunately." He laughed.

She smiled. "Don't they all?"

"Women." He shook his head. "Waddya gonna do?" He looked at Samantha with a twinkle in his eye.

Each took a few minutes to process the information about the other.

Strollo broke the silence. "What about your husband, Chip's dad?"

"He was about ten years older than me. In his twenties he raced cars. He's a lawyer, and as he prospered he bought a new car every year and traded in the old ones."

"What happened?"

"Like his cars, he decided to trade me in on a newer model. Except he didn't tell me. I had to find out when everyone else did."

"What a jerk."

"Yeah. He's taken care of Chip and me money-wise. I have to say that for him. I wish he would spend more time with the boy, though."

"He's a handsome young man. The girls must fall all over him."

"They do and he loves women." She laughed.

"Do you give him advice about women?"

"Yes."

"Does he pay any attention to your advice?"

"Of course not." They both laughed.

Another silence as they each took a sip of wine.

"I've never done this before," she said.

"What?"

"Invited a man over late in the evening to feed him."

"Neither have I," he said. "I never invite men over to feed them. I'm a terrible cook."

She jumped up. "I'll be right back."

Strollo looked out the window and studied the western sky. The stars were visible since there was no moon. He took a deep breath and felt good. He wasn't sure if it was the chicken noodle soup, the wine, or Samantha: perhaps all three. He was sure of one thing: he felt better than he had felt in a long time.

He heard a noise and glanced at the open double doors. Samantha wore a purple silk bathrobe, her black hair sparkling with droplets from a quick shower. Her impish grin made her look like a teenage girl. "How would you like some desert?"

He jumped up and bumped his shin on the coffee table. "Ouch!"

"Are you OK?"

"Yeah, I'm fine."

He limped to her, staring into to those deep brown eyes, smelling her perfume moments before kissing her. His hands moved down her sides and rested on her firm bottom. He pulled her to him.

"It's been too long since a man touched me like that." Samantha panted. "Come on, Louis, there's a room I haven't shown you yet—my bedroom."

—⁓—

Strollo woke up in an unfamiliar place. *Where am I?* He looked around and soon comprehended the reality that he had been sleeping in Samantha's bed, immersed in pillows and fluffy blankets. She lay next to him with her head propped up by one arm, smiling. "Good morning, Detective. I'll say this, you sure know how to get to the bottom of things."

He pulled her to him and cuddled her. "And what a bottom it is."

Samantha pressed her long fingers against his back as if holding him in place to keep him from falling away from her. "I'm so tired of being alone."

"So am I." Strollo took a deep breath. "I just have one question."

"What?"

"Are there seconds on desserts?"

"I like a man who knows what he wants."

She pulled the covers over them, and lips, tongues, fingers, arms, and legs fought frantically to become entwined.

Chapter 9

PICKLER PROBED

A few days later, Pickler arrived at the police station for his ten o'clock meeting. They sat at Strollo's conference table after exchanging pleasantries.

"Thanks for coming today, Carl. I think you can help with some things I'm working on."

"Sure, Louie. I'll help anyway I can."

"On the first of April, you came into the office after hours. Why did you do that?"

"Why does that date seem familiar?"

"That's the night a cab driver was slain."

"Oh no! Are you accusing me of killing the cab driver? I'm getting a lawyer." Pickler pushed away from the table, preparing to get up.

"You're welcome to get a lawyer. I'm only looking for information. I'm exploring the possibility of a relationship between the murderer and Briggs News 20."

Pickler sat back down and breathed a sigh of relief. "OK. You know, this hasn't been a stellar year for me."

"I know. From what I've heard, you got the shaft." Strollo got up from his desk and opened a small refrigerator where he had half liters of bottled water and soft drinks. "Want something to drink?"

"I'll take one of those Diet Cokes."

Strollo took out a Diet Coke and a Dr. Pepper for himself. He handed Pickler the soda pop and eased into a chair at the conference room table.

"Let's start over. Why did you go back to the office on the night of April first?"

"I forgot my laptop. I needed it the next morning for a live shot." He took a sip from his Diet Coke.

"Did you see anyone else at the office?"

"I don't recall seeing anyone. I was in a hurry to get the computer and go home."

"How would you describe your relationship with Thomas Whitherspoon and Leon Rump?"

"Didn't know Rump all that well; he kept to himself. He was friendlier with Whitherspoon, than with me. They've been colleagues for many years. Tom was my mentor. Or at least I thought he was. After I resigned Rump told my wife that Whitherspoon had been out to get me—I guess he was hell-bent on taking me down."

"Why?"

"Thought I was out for his job according to Rump—which I wasn't," Pickler said. "I looked up to Whitherspoon as someone I could learn from."

"What about the newspaper article accusing a Briggs News 20 anchor of racism?"

"The racist accusations were bogus. Rump told my wife he thought Whitherspoon planted them."

"I'll do everything I can to help clear your name. I know you don't have a racist bone in your body."

"That's what I've been saying all along, but no one believes me, Lou." He took another sip.

"Did anything strange happen at the station that night? Anything at all?"

"Not really. I wish I could be more help."

"OK, Carl. Thanks for coming down."

Pickler left. Strollo retreated to his desk and called the lab. "Can you get up here right away? I have the samples for you. He abandoned them so we can use them for evidence."

A few minutes later a man wearing rubber gloves and a lab coat popped in the office.

"It's over there." Strollo pointed at the Diet Coke. "Can you get the DNA sample and fingerprints from that?"

"We should be able to. I'll let you know for sure after we've completed our tests." He swabbed the mouth of the can, stuck the sample in a sterile plastic bag then put the can in a sealed plastic container and left.

Chapter 10

INTERVIEWS

Strollo and Samantha met in her office to interview Rump and Whitherspoon about why they came to the TV station after hours on the night of the first murder. Whitherspoon had returned to work a few days before but had not resumed work on the nightly newscast.

"I did some maintenance work on the switcher in the control room. It can be done only when we've shut down for the night." Leon Rump fidgeted in his chair and flipped his ponytail away from his back to straighten it out. "After the last newscast, I got some dinner and came back to work on it."

"The TV station's security cameras were disabled that day. Why?" Strollo looked directly into Rump's eyes as if reading a book.

"I've been having trouble with those cameras for six months now. For no reason they reset. I just haven't had time to take them apart and see what's wrong." Rump shook his head. "It's a bitch."

"Did you see anyone else?" Detective Strollo asked.

Rump peered at Samantha, unsuccessfully trying to read her expression. "Kingpin must've come into the building, I saw his car in the lot. Didn't talk to him, though—probably making calls from his cubicle."

"If you didn't talk to him, how did you know that?" Strollo asked.

"'Cause he usually makes calls when he comes in after hours."

"To whom?"

"I dunno. Just calls. You'll have to ask him."

Strollo rolled his pen back and forward between his thumb and forefinger. "Did you observe anything out of the ordinary in the building, other than Whitherspoon working late?"

Rocking back in his chair, eyes glancing around as if in thought, Rump replied, "No, Detective. Nothing I can think of. I can't even tell you what I had for lunch yesterday." He chuckled.

"OK. That'll be all. Thanks." Strollo nodded.

Rump's breathing grew rapid. "What's this about?"

"Nothing concerning you." Samantha rose and opened her door. "Please don't say anything about this meeting."

He got up from the chair and left without another word.

Samantha closed the door and turned to face Strollo. Their eyes met. Strollo moved closer to her, within kissing distance. She dropped her arms to her sides and waited for him to hug and kiss her. At the last second, he veered off and sat down.

Samantha pouted and returned to her desk with a troubled look on her face. "What's with you?"

"I'm here to investigate a homicide, not to pursue our romantic relationship."

"Well, goodie-goodie for you. Aren't you the wonderful law enforcement professional."

They both laughed.

Next, Samantha dialed Whitherspoon. "Tom, could you please come down here for a few minutes? Thanks."

Fifteen minutes later, Whitherspoon sat in a chair opposite Strollo at her conference table. Samantha remained at her desk.

Strollo's hands were folded on the desk in front of him. "Tom, thanks for coming here on short notice. I heard you had been in the hospital for a few days—hope you're feeling better."

"Yeah. It was nothing. They just wanted to run some tests before releasing me. Jocko wants me to work in the office for a week or so before going back on air. I'm just fine, but thanks for asking."

"Glad to hear it. I'm investigating some crimes that may be connected to people working here. On the night of April first, the security card reader reported you came in after hours. What were you doing?"

"Calling around for agents. Not happy with the one I had. I wanted to get somebody to handle negotiations when my current contract is up."

"Did you see anyone else in the building?"

"No."

"How long were you at the station?"

"A little over an hour."

"Did you notice anything odd?" Strollo sucked on the end of his pen.

Whitherspoon glanced at the ceiling, then back at Strollo. "I can't think of anything. Sorry. Hey, wait. That was the night of the first murder. You don't think I had something to do with it, do you?"

"Not at all."

Whitherspoon rubbed his thumb in circles on his forefinger. "Then why are you asking?"

"Take it easy, Tom." Samantha interjected. "Detective Strollo thought you might have some helpful information. First and foremost you're a newsman and a former reporter, which means your powers of observation and questioning mind can uncover facts others miss."

Whitherspoon puffed up at the compliment and sat up a little straighter. *Samantha's a jewel. She gets me.* "Oh, now I see where you're coming from. I didn't see anyone or anything abnormal. I was there an hour and a half at the most and left."

"OK, Tom. That's all for now. Thanks." Strollo put his pen on the table and got up off the chair.

Whitherspoon got up and nodded in return. "Detective. See you, Samantha."

"Bye, Tom. Keep quiet about this little talk. Thanks."

After Whitherspoon left, Strollo put his hands in his pockets and stared at the floor. "Well, those interviews didn't help much. I hoped we'd get more things we could use."

Samantha rested her chin on her palm. "A couple of things, Louis. The security card report showed Pickler came in first, then Whitherspoon, followed by Rump. None of them were at the station at the same time."

"So Rump lied. He couldn't have seen Whitherspoon—'cause he wasn't here."

"Right. He stayed over two hours—but why would he lie about seeing Whitherspoon?" she asked.

"Good question. He may be confused with another night, or if he knows we're investigating theft from the TV station that night, he's offering up another suspect. Was anything stolen around that time?"

Samantha shook her head. "Not that I know of, but we don't do inventory until the end of the year."

"Here's a thought—Rump could have been in the building to steal something that night and to plan a murder."

"But why would he kill a cab driver he didn't even know?"

"Why would anyone kill a cab driver he didn't know?" Strollo asked.

She folded her arms. "We have more questions than answers."

"Yeah, the results of the DNA and fingerprint tests should be enlightening."

—⁊⁊—

At the other end of the building, Martin bounded into Rump's engineering shop and plopped on one of the workbench stools. "There you are, Uncle Leon. I've looked all over the place for you."

"Been meeting with Samantha and Detective Strollo." He reached for a sandwich from his cooler. "You want one?"

"No, thanks. What'd they want?"

"Nothing. Just some questions—wanted to know why on a certain day I came into the office after hours to work late. Wouldn't say why, but probably had something to do with stealing going on at the station. Equipment's been turning up missing and I reported it to Jocko."

"Did my name come up?"

"No. Sure you don't want a tuna sandwich?" He reached into his cooler and held out another sandwich.

"Yeah. I'm good. If Strollo comes in again, let me know," Martin said. "He's my contact at the police department for the murder investigations, and he's avoiding me."

"Sure. You got it." Rump took another big bite of his sandwich. Stray pieces of it tumbled from each corner of his mouth. "Why're you looking for me?"

"Need some advice. Since Kingpin got out of the hospital, he seems different. Can't put my finger on it. Do you think he's up to something?"

"What d'ya mean?" Rump asked.

"He's a real jerk, but since he got back he's been nice—too nice. I expected some push back when he found out Jocko had put me in charge of covering the homicide investigations."

"Doesn't mean he's not pissed at you." Rump pointed the last fragment of his sandwich at Martin then popped it in his mouth.

"True. He's not just saying nice things, though—he's *acting* nice."

"If he's acting nice, look out. He's up to something," Rump said.

"Yeah, I thought the same thing," Martin said. "But what?"

Rump finished off a bottle of iced tea and wiped his mouth with a paper towel. "Here's all you need to know about Kingpin— flatter him and you can get him to do almost anything for you. He's a sucker for praise. Play to his ego, get him to open up, and you'll find out what he's up to."

"Good advice. Thanks, Uncle Leon."

—m—

The next day, Samantha entered the studio as Charles Buck and Stephanie packed their gear. "How'd the shoot go?"

Charles paused and straightened up from his camera case. "According to plan. We got the samples from all of the on-air talent, and we didn't mess with Rump's ponytail either. We'll take everything directly to the police lab for processing."

"Good. Thanks a lot. Call if you need anything. You can send the photo disc to Jocko." Samantha waved and left.

A few minutes later, Whitherspoon's head popped in the doorway. When he observed an empty studio except for the photographers, he ventured in. "May I speak with the lady for a few minutes?"

Charles nodded and continued packing up his light stands.

Stephanie eyed Whitherspoon. "What can I do for you?"

"I apologize for the way I spoke to you the last time you were here. I feel bad about my rude and obnoxious language, and boorish behavior."

She nodded. "OK. Thanks."

Chapter 11

HELPING OTHERS

"But, Jocko, I didn't have a heart attack. You were at the hospital. We talked about it. They ran more tests and everything's looking good. No heart damage. They think stress may have had something to do with it," Whitherspoon pleaded. "I'm ready to go back on the air."

"Sorry, Tom. I feel it's best for you to take some time off, at least a couple of months, so your health can stabilize. If it's stress-related, we can't put you back on news. That's a pressure cooker."

"But the docs say I'm in good health," Whitherspoon said. "I can have them call you or send a letter. Which do you want?"

"I want you healthy, and a couple of months off will do you good," Jocko said.

"Would you be saying that if I was thirty?" Whitherspoon glared at Jocko.

"Sure. It's not about your age. It's about your health."

"Who'll anchor 'The Good News Show'?" Whitherspoon asked.

"Rex. We'll go with a single-anchor format. Good News airs on Fridays. He'll have time to do that and still cover the murder investigations. Carol Lackey can help out."

"But she's *my* producer."

"She's the *station's* producer," Jocko corrected.

"If you say so, boss. But I'm fine. Anyway, I *need* to get back to work." He reached his hand into his pocket and squeezed his car keys into his palm.

"You *need* to get your health back. You're on paid leave for two months, and that's final." Jocko pointed at Whitherspoon. "One more thing. Your office remodel will be done by the time you return. I want you to share it with Rex. That will facilitate stronger communications and help us stay on budget."

Whitherspoon looked at the floor for a few seconds and sighed. "OK. See you in a couple of months." He raced out of the building, jumped into his Porsche, and roared down the street. He drove to the home of the first slain cab driver Manuel Dominguez.

—m—

Carmaletta Dominguez heard a knock at her front door. She looked through the peephole and saw a tall, distinguished-looking man standing there. She recognized him as the local news anchor and opened the door a crack but kept the chain locked. "Yes?"

"Mrs. Dominguez, I'm Tom Whitherspoon from Briggs News 20. May I come in?"

"I've already told the police everything I know, Mr. Whitherspoon."

"I'm not here about the investigation. I wanted to see how you're doing."

"Come on in." She unlocked the chain and gestured toward the kitchen table. They walked through the living room, an obstacle course filled with dozens of toy trucks and cars of various sizes and a rainbow of other toys. Her sons were still in their pajamas, mesmerized by a TV program about space aliens.

"Mr. Whitherspoon, I'd like you to meet my sons, Jamie and Jason." She looked at them and pointed. "Jamie's seven and Jason is five."

"Hey, guys, what's up?"

They looked in his direction and smiled. Jason waved then looked back at the TV.

Whitherspoon dodged and sidestepped his way through the maze of little vehicles without crushing anything in his path. The kitchen, by contrast, was immaculate: no dirty dishes in the sink, the countertop clean and free of clutter, the kitchen table shiny, and the floor waxed.

"I'm sorry for your loss. Everything I've heard about your husband has increased my respect for him. Briggs News 20 is running an anonymous tip line crawl at the bottom of our newscasts to solicit leads from the community in case anyone has information leading to an arrest and prosecution."

At that moment, the younger boy, Jason, came into the kitchen and held up a book on spacemen in Whitherspoon's direction.

Leaning down to the boy, Whitherspoon smiled. "Oh yeah. Spacemen. I like them too. You want me to read it to you?"

"No. My Daddy bought me this book. He'll read it to me." He turned and carried the book back into the living room and resumed watching TV, still holding the book in his arms.

Carmaletta looked away for a few moments then back at Whitherspoon. "Manny was a fine man and I miss him so much. It breaks my heart to think that my boys will grow up without their father. But, everyone has treated us with such kindness, especially our church. Would you like to sit down and let me get you a cup of coffee?"

"Sure. Black. No cream or sugar."

"You got it." She walked over to the cupboard and opened the door, revealing cups and glasses lined up with such precision that they looked like a military formation. Finding a large blue mug, she poured him a cup and refilled her own, and then replaced the pot, before joining him at the table.

Whitherspoon noticed that her flowered dress flowed with every step, her movements as organized as her cupboard. "Mrs. Dominguez, how are *you* doing?"

"We're OK for now. Manny had a life insurance policy, which will give us a few months of living expenses. But I'm going to have to go back to work to support us." She took a long sip from her coffee mug and looked over the top of it at Whitherspoon.

He looked into her brown eyes as he spoke. "Well, look. I want to help. I'm going to write you a check for a thousand dollars. Then I'm going to send you monthly checks until you get back on your feet. Don't tell a soul," Whitherspoon said.

"That's nice of you, sir, but I can't accept that amount of money from you."

"I make good money. I can afford it."

"That's very generous of you, Mr. Whitherspoon, but you don't have to do that. I trust in the good Lord to take care of us."

"Did you ever think that the good Lord could be taking care of you through me?"

Carmaletta looked down, gripping her mug in both hands as tears rained out of both eyes and dripped on the table. She wiped the running mascara with her fingertips.

Whitherspoon pulled out his checkbook from a lapel pocket and wrote a check for a thousand dollars and held it out to her. "Here you go."

She took the check. "Thanks, but—I don't know what to say." She reached for a paper towel and blotted her cheeks.

"You don't need to say anything. Here's my card. If you need something, call." He set his business card on the kitchen table and got up. "Thanks for the coffee. It tasted delicious."

"You're quite welcome."

"Say, I'll be taking a couple months off work, but I'll be around town for a while before I leave. Do you think you sons would like to go to a ball game?"

"They'd love it."

"OK. I'll be calling you to arrange it as soon as I check the park schedule." He extended his hand to shake.

Carmaletta rose to her feet and shook his hand. Then she threw her arms around him. "Thanks, Mr. Whitherspoon. Thanks a lot."

—⚬—

A couple of days later, Whitherspoon took care of more unfinished business.

"So, Jocko gave you a couple months off. What are you going to do with yourself—spend some serious 'me time' in front of the mirror?" Carol Lackey smiled and drank some water. She and Whitherspoon had just placed their dinner orders at Guido's Italian restaurant, her favorite. She loved their homemade lasagna, and Whitherspoon had promised for years that someday he'd take her there. Someday finally came.

"Work around the house, probably go to Denver and Wyoming for a time. Got some unfinished business," Whitherspoon said.

"Why? Need a hair implant?"

"Do I have to pay extra for the jokes? Sorry. It's personal. But I appreciate your interest in my follicles. They're doing fine, thank you very much. I'm touched by your concern for my personal life. I realize compared with yours, mine must seem quite exciting." Whitherspoon grinned as he waited for her comeback.

"Oh, it's exciting watching your life up close—like watching a train wreck. Natural disasters have always fascinated me," Carol said.

"On a serious note, speaking of my life, you saved it by calling nine-one-one. I can't thank you enough, Carol."

"You told folks on the staff it wasn't a heart attack, so I couldn't have saved your life."

"You did. Let's leave it at that." Whitherspoon raised his wineglass. "A toast to one of my oldest and dearest friends, Carol Lackey."

She raised her glass and touched his. "Do you mind if we edit out the 'oldest' part and keep in the 'dearest' part?"

"OK, to the dearest and most hypersensitive-about-her-age colleague I know."

"Speaking of age, didn't you tint your hair by age twenty-two?" Carol asked.

"Yeah, about the same time you joined *Weight Watchers*. You've been with them so long, you probably don't even pay dues."

"I don't. I'm a lifetime member, so with the money I've saved, I can buy you a gift. Do you want a cane or a walker?"

"Definitely a cane. I need something to beat the women off."

"There's only one thing women find attractive about old fogies like you—their wallets."

They both chuckled, and every head in Guido's jerked in their direction.

"Carol." Whitherspoon lowered his voice and looked into her eyes.

"What?" She set both hands palms down on the table as if bracing herself for what was coming next.

"You have green eyes. I never noticed that before," he said.

"Yes, Tom. All my life."

He put his left hand on her right hand, which rested next to her wineglass. "There's something I want to ask you."

She smiled and looked down at their hands. "Go ahead."

"When I'm in Colorado, will you help Rex put on 'The Good News Show'? Make him look good."

"Sure. I'll take care of Rex." She kept smiling as she pulled her hand out from under his and tapped it on the tabletop. "Can't wait till they bring that lasagna. I'm starved."

—⁓—

Crack! The aluminum bat pinged as it launched the softball high in the air. Two outfielders raced from opposite directions in chase of its trajectory until one waved off the other, snatching the missile with an over-the-head grab. Game over.

The bleachers erupted with cheers. Hannah Strollo had notched another victory with a ten-strikeout performance in the Briggs Lake summer softball league. Arizona State head coach Tito Alvarez had driven from Tempe to recruit her to play for the Sun Devils. "This Strollo girl is the real deal," he said to himself.

A mob of teammates, bouncing up and down, surrounded the star pitcher. Hannah clutched her glove in her left hand. Her cap had been knocked off by a congratulatory group hug and hung lifelessly from her right hand. She scanned the bleachers, hoping to see her dad. *Dad could have made it after all and wants to surprise me.* Her eyes settled on Coach Alvarez as he made his way through the crowd. *That must be the coach.*

"Good game, Hannah," he said. "I'm Coach Alvarez. You controlled that team from the first inning, and your fastball seemed to pick up heat with each inning." He extended a hand. "Glad to meet you."

"Pleased to meet you, Coach Alvarez. Thanks for the compliment. I'm sure you could tell it was a team effort all the way."

"You did your part. That's for sure. Is your father here?"

Hannah's eyes searched the ballpark again. *Oh, Daddy, why couldn't you be here?* "No. He couldn't make it, Coach. There's been a couple of murders, and he's a homicide detective." She shrugged.

"I understand." Coach Alvarez removed his cap to wipe sweat from his forehead. "We want you to come to the campus in September—spend the weekend, meet some of our softball players. How does that sound?"

"Great!"

Carl and Marlene snaked their way through the crowd of fans to the exuberant team celebration. "Good game, Hannah," Carl said.

"Thanks."

"You were lights out today, lady," Marlene added, lifting their baby toward Hannah. "Even Cooper stayed awake." As if on cue, Cooper smiled and made a little fist.

"Glad to hear it, Mrs. Pickler. Cooper's adorable." She gave the baby a gentle fist touch. Turning to the coach, she gestured toward the Picklers. "This is Mr. and Mrs. Pickler and their son, Cooper."

Coach Alvarez waved. "I know the Picklers well. They're alumni and Marlene's in our hall of fame. We called her the 'Blond Bomber.' She led us to two league championships as our catcher and cleanup batter—a real power hitter."

"I called her the blond bombshell," Carl quipped.

Hannah's eyebrows arched. "Mrs. Pickler, you never told me you were a softball star!"

Marlene smiled. "Ancient history."

"So long. Gotta get my hall-of-fame wife some dinner," Pickler said with a smile. "Her head is swelling by the minute."

"Good seeing you guys," Coach Alvarez said.

As Pickler ushered his wife to their car, he came face-to-face with Whitherspoon. The surprise stopped Pickler in his tracks. Marlene looked the other way when she saw Whitherspoon and continued walking toward the car carrying Cooper.

Stunned to see Whitherspoon at the game wearing cargo shorts and flip-flops, Pickler couldn't help smiling. *He's even wearing a baseball cap. He's gonna mess up his perfect hair.* "What're you doing here?"

"Hi, Carl! Good game, huh?" Whitherspoon said.

"I didn't know you were into women's softball."

"There's a lot you don't know about me." Smiling, he put both hands in his pockets.

Carl stopped smiling. "Are you OK? I heard you're on medical leave."

"Nothing serious. I'm fine. But thanks for asking. Pick, I'm sorry about what happened to you at the station, and if I could ever—"

"I'll keep that in mind." Glancing in the direction of his wife, who continued walking to their car, "Excuse me. I gotta catch up with Marlene. Nice seeing you." He hurried toward the parking lot to catch up with her.

When he caught up to Marlene, she made a face. "What's with you? That's the guy who got you fired. Have you forgotten? How can you stand there and talk to him like that?"

He offered no answers, and she didn't expect any. These were rhetorical questions: her way of reminding her husband not to give an emotional pass to Whitherspoon.

Whitherspoon turned his attention to the concession stand. Jamie and Jason had wanted more snacks before going home, so he had given them a twenty-dollar bill. He saw the boys running his way with big smiles and arms filled with goodies. "Hey, guys, looks like you scored."

Jamie, the seven-year-old, spoke. "Yes, Mr. Whitherspoon. Jason even got a free pretzel because they were packing up." He pointed at his five-year-old brother, bringing up the rear, juggling bags of candy.

"You guys can sure eat. I'll say that for you." Whitherspoon put his arm on Jamie's shoulder and accepted a box of Milk Duds from Jason. "Thanks, dude. C'mon, we gotta see the coach." He shepherded the boys to the parking lot to intercept Coach Alvarez.

"Excuse me. I saw you talking with Hannah Strollo," Whitherspoon said. "I recognized you from seeing an interview you did with Ronnie Gaboni for a Briggs News sports segment."

Coach Alvarez stopped and eyed the tall stranger with the two young boys in tow. "Yes?"

"Hannah's father couldn't be here. He's the chief homicide detective here in Briggs Lake, and he's investigating a couple of high profile murders. He raised her by himself after his wife died of cancer. Detective Strollo's a man of integrity and honor who's respected in our community. His daughter's the same way. They're good people. Thought you should know. They're class acts."

"Thanks. Good to know. We're looking for good athletes, but we're also looking for good people: students with character," replied Alvarez. "These your boys?"

"No. They're my buds." Whitherspoon looked over at Jamie and Jason, who were posing like a couple of choirboys at church. The sight made him smile and he yelled, "Let's go guys." With a nod to Coach Alvarez, the three pals sauntered toward their car.

After strapping the boys into their seats, Whitherspoon fired up the Porsche. "You guys are good—real charmers."

"Waddya mean?" Jamie asked.

"You wouldn't stay put all day. You scampered all over this ballpark and wore me to a frazzle keeping up with you, then in front of Coach you stand still like a couple of angels."

Jamie looked puzzled. "Is that bad?"

"No." Whitherspoon smiled. "It was good and I was proud of you. Your mom will never let me take you to a game again if I don't get you home soon. Don't even think of spilling anything on my nice clean seats, or you'll be sorry."

When Carmaletta opened her front door, the boys ran in, chattering about the game and showing off the souvenirs Whitherspoon had purchased. "It's late. Get up to your rooms and put your jammies on. It's way past your bedtimes. Say thank you to Mr. Whitherspoon."

"Thanks, Mr. Whitherspoon," said Jamie.

Jason walked up to Whitherspoon and put his arms around his leg. "Tanks."

They scrambled up the stairs.

Carmaletta and Whitherspoon, alone in the foyer for the first time, studied each other closely.

He noticed that she wore makeup and pink lipstick. Her flowered blouse matched her orange shorts, which were modest but tight enough to reveal her trim figure.

She smiled at him. "In your baseball cap and shorts, you look so much different from that guy we see on our TV—much taller too. Thank you so much, Tom. They needed that."

"I needed that too. It was fun hanging out with them—good boys. I always wanted a son, but my ex-wife and I couldn't have children."

"Please come in. I've just brewed a fresh pot of coffee for you." She searched his eyes.

"Sorry, I can't. I have stuff to do. Another time?"

She stopped smiling and looked down. "Sure. Thanks for everything, Mr. Whitherspoon. Take care." She remained in the doorway and watched as he drove off.

Chapter 12

FANNIE AMBUSHES RUMP

Fannie Larsen showed up unannounced at Briggs News 20. The receptionist escorted her to Rump's workshop without calling him first, since Fannie had worked at the station last summer.

At the sight of her, Rump felt blood rushing to his face. Dropping the wiring from a playback deck in need of repair, he wiped his hands with a nearby rag. "What're you doing here, Fannie?"

"Surprised to see me?" Fannie's short blond hair shimmered with frosted highlights. She wore a short, white, mid-thigh skirt with material so thin it almost seemed transparent, and Rump could see the outline of her muscles as she walked. Her pink blouse with black polka dots displayed enough cleavage to distract him from looking her in the eye while talking to her—the view below too tempting.

"I've called three times and left messages. I've texted you, sent e-mails and a card. Why won't you get back to me?" A red-faced Fannie Larsen spoke in rapid bursts like a .50-caliber machine gun. "What the hell's going on, you weenie?"

"I've been busy," Rump said.

"Too busy to make a phone call?" She put her hands on her hips. "Pul-eese. Give me a friggin' break."

"Lotsa stuff going on here," Rump answered.

"Yeah? Well, I got lots of stuff going on too. You promised to make me a demo reel and get me a job in broadcasting. Now you're blowing me off. I'm not a happy camper, Leon."

"Sorry, Fannie."

"Sorry my ass!"

"Whitherspoon had a heart attack. He's out at least two months. When he gets back, he'll get you a job."

"OK," she said. "I'll give you a couple of months, but then I want action."

"Sure. Not a problem."

Fannie walked to the door of Rump's workshop, then closed and locked it. Turning back, she marched to within a foot of him. "Just so you know—if you don't follow through this time, I'm going to the authorities. I'll tell them how you stripped me naked and had your way with me in the front seat of your Suburban. I'm sure the police would love to hear all about it."

"Fannie, it was consensual sex." He rubbed his palms on the sides of his pants. "That's all it was. Nothing more."

Fannie jabbed the center of his chest with her finger. "You raped me, asshole!"

"We had an arrangement. You asked me to do some things for you, and I asked you to do some things for me."

"That's not the way it went down. I'll tell the police you took a naive coed out for dinner, got her drunk, and took advantage of her. You screwed her in the front seat of your Suburban. I'm no lawyer, but I'm sure you'll do jail time, you dirty old man."

Rump felt the hot blast of air from her mouth on his face. He smelled her minty breath, and her perfume overpowered him. He grabbed her shoulders and kissed her.

After the long kiss, she pushed him away. "You horny old bastard!"

"You whore!"

"You can't get enough of this stuff, can you?" She smiled, her face still wet with his saliva. "That should give you a little motivation. Now, get your fat ass in gear."

Fannie turned her back on Rump and swaggered toward the door, her arms swinging from side to side. When she got to the door, she unlocked it and looked back at him. "You've got two months." She slammed the door on her way out.

Rump reached for his cell phone and dialed Whitherspoon.

"Whitherspoon here."

"Hey, Kingpin, it's Leon. How ya feelin'?"

"Never felt so good in my whole life."

"Glad to hear it. Say, I got a visit today from Fannie Larsen, the intern from last summer."

"Sure. How's she doing?"

"Fine. Except she wants me to get working on her demo reel and wants you to get her a job in broadcasting."

"You know I'm on leave for a couple of months," Whitherspoon said. "Did you tell her I'm out of the office?"

"I told her that," Rump said. "But she's real pushy. She even threatened you."

"Threatened me? With what?"

"With going to Samantha to tell her that she lied about Pickler's racism. She'll say you and me set Pick up."

Whitherspoon took a deep breath.

"Did you hear what I said?" Rump asked.

"Yeah. I'm thinking...how'd she know I was involved with the Pickler scheme?"

"I dunno. I didn't tell her. Just said you'd recommend her for a job. She musta figured the rest out on her own."

"What a mess."

Rump sighed. "I know. That's why I'm calling. What're we going to do now?"

"Well, for starters, *you* better get a demo reel put together for her and recommend her to *your* contacts," Whitherspoon said.

131

"Yeah. I'll go to Arizona State and edit her on-air highlights on a DVD. Then she won't think you're avoiding her."

"Me? Wait a minute, Leon. How come I keep getting interjected into this? I'm not avoiding anyone. You're the one talking to her, and if promises were made, you made them, not me. You own this. You're the one that has to fix this."

"Yeah. Sure. But you'll get her a job, right?" Rump said.

"I didn't promise her I'd get her a job. Did *you* promise her you'd get her a job?" Whitherspoon asked.

"No, but she thinks I did, which is kinda the same thing."

"I thought you told her we would help market her demo to prospective employers and I'd recommend her to some contacts. You know we can't promise anyone a job."

"Well, based on what she said today, she thinks we promised her a job," Rump said. "That's all I know."

"That's absurd," Whitherspoon said. "I couldn't promise my own mother a job!"

"Like it or not, that's what she thinks. She's serious about going to Samantha. We gotta do something fast, Kingpin. This could get real ugly."

"Get her reel done and explain we didn't promise her a job. We'll recommend her to some contacts. That's all we can do. I gotta go. Keep me posted."

Chapter 13

BAPTISM BRUNCH

This particular Sunday was a special day for the Picklers They enjoyed a brunch with Detective Strollo after the baptism ceremony for their son, Cooper. They sat opposite Strollo in the booth, the baby between them in his infant seat.

"Thanks for supporting Cooper and our family on his special day," Pickler said. "It was an amazing baptism ceremony, and your presence made it even more memorable."

"I'm honored to be his godfather. You've both supported Hannah. It's the least I can do." *This is so awkward. I'm sitting with a man who could have killed two innocent people and his wife. I have to pretend we're buddy-buddy while I'm putting clues together that could put him in prison for life.*

"We love watching her pitch," Marlene said. "Best of all, Hannah's a fine person."

"Takes after her dad," Carl said.

Strollo took a sip of his coffee. *Yeah, this fine person could be sending you to the slammer. I never thought acting would be part of my detective job description.*

"The other day, I received a call from the head coach of Arizona State, Tito Alvarez. He said one of my friends gave Hannah and me a top recommendation. I know it was you guys, and I want you to know it meant the world to us."

"A brief conversation, Lou. Nothing more." Marlene said.

"Something you said convinced Coach she had the personal integrity to go with the softball talent. He's offered Hannah a four-year athletic scholarship."

"That's wonderful news. We're so happy for you and Hannah," Carl said. He turned to Marlene. "I have to give all the credit to my wife. They couldn't resist a recommendation from their hall-of-fame catcher." He put his arm around her.

"I didn't share anything about you or Hannah," Marlene said, blushing. "Hannah got the scholarship on her own. She has the talent, and she has the character. No doubt."

"Yeah, I know. But Coach said that a friend chased him down in the parking lot and mentioned my integrity and character and how I raised her." Strollo smiled at the thought. "I could never have been able to afford the cost of sending her to college. This is so great." He wiped his hands on his napkin.

The Picklers glanced at each other, and Carl's expression told Marlene it wasn't him who talked to the coach.

He turned his gaze on Strollo. "I think your reputation precedes you. We didn't say anything, but it's true—you're a good man who's raised a fine daughter."

"You Picklers are way too humble. Anyway, thanks."

"Forget it," Carl said.

Strollo took a deep breath and looked away from the couple and down at Cooper. "He sure is a cute kid. Is he going to follow in his parents' footsteps and be a ballplayer?"

"I think that's a pretty safe bet," Marlene said.

They laughed, still studying the little baby in front of them, until Marlene tugged at her husband's shirt sleeve. "Carl, tell Lou your idea."

Pickler finished his coffee and set the empty mug on the table. "I'm good friends with Hannah's high school coach, and we're going to work with her team to do a series of fund-raisers that will benefit the families of Manuel Dominguez and Chico Escobar.

We've already had one meeting with the girls, and they're excited to help."

"Wonderful idea. They're a special group of girls who really care about each other." Strollo looked around the restaurant for a few seconds. "Well, I should be going."

Carl nodded. "Yeah, and we need to get Cooper home. He's had a lot of excitement today, and it's about time for his nap." He called the waitress over to take a digital picture of them before they split up.

—⁂—

On the way home, Carl drove to a scenic overlook where they liked to talk. It boasted a great view of a mountain range in the distance that framed a valley of rock formations and desert landscape. He parked and kept the engine running so they could enjoy the panorama. Cooper, asleep in his infant carrier in the backseat, made tiny snoring sounds as he breathed.

Marlene leaned her head on his shoulder and sighed. "This place is so relaxing. It sure has been a great day."

"Whitherspoon," he said.

"What?"

"Whitherspoon."

She lifted her head and turned to face him. "What're you talking about? You've got Whitherspoon on the brain, dear boy."

"At the game. Whitherspoon was at the game."

"And that means what?"

"That means Whitherspoon told Coach Alvarez how great Louie and Hannah are. It must have been him. We didn't say anything about them." He stared at Marlene, waiting for her to comprehend the meaning of what he had just said.

"You're right. He must have. But why? That man doesn't do anything for anybody but himself. He's working some angle, you can be sure of that."

"Do you think his health crisis changed him?"

"People don't change that much, Carl. You're such an idealist. That's one of the things I love about you, though." She put her hand on the side of his head and kissed him. "You're such a good man."

He held her close.

"Waaaaaaa! Waaaaa!" came a loud cry from the backseat.

"Oops. I guess we woke sleeping beauty," Marlene said. "Time to put Cooper down for a nap."

"Yeah."

"And when I'm finished with Coop, how would you like to have me put *you* down for a nap?"

He didn't need to answer, his smiling face said it all.

Chapter 14

JOURNEY TO THE PAST

Whitherspoon spent the rest of July getting his house in order. First on the list was getting rid of his pornographic magazines. He completed long-delayed projects in the basement, including a remodel of his rec room/man cave. He sifted through old files and tossed them to purge himself of the old Whitherspoon. He put his photo albums on DVDs and scanned all his important documents. He avoided watching TV, especially Briggs News 20. He couldn't bear to watch the nightly news delivered by Rex Martin. As August approached, he decided to do some traveling with the last month of his leave: first stop Denver.

—w—

"Go, Broncos!" Whitherspoon turned to the man on his left. "What a game!"

Nick Dosh nodded in agreement. "That's for sure."

Nick's wife, Naomi, sat on his left. Whitherspoon and Dosh had two things in common: they loved the Denver Broncos, and both had married Naomi.

Naomi leaned forward, looking at Whitherspoon, "Tom, I don't know how you got us such good seats to a Denver Broncos preseason game, but we're grateful."

"I still have a few good contacts in Denver. They don't call me the Kingpin for nothing." He smiled. Then turning to her husband, he said, "Nick, I hope that didn't come across as egotistical. I meant—"

"I know what you meant." Nick continued to concentrate on the playing field while speaking. "The Broncos have such a knack for scoring quickly, you always think they have a good chance to win, even when they're behind."

"True." Whitherspoon added, "That's one of the things I love about 'em—they never quit. This is a preseason game in August, and they're playing like it's the Super Bowl. Say, how's the PR biz?"

"To be honest Tom, I got laid off. They called it 'restructuring'—not about my age, they said, but I think age had something to do with it." He shrugged and looked at Whitherspoon. "What're you gonna do?"

"Companies all do that stuff, but never admit it 'cause they don't wanna be sued for age discrimination," Whitherspoon said. "Same in broadcast news. I'm scrambling my butt off to stay ahead of these young studs who are out for my job. It happens in pro football too. Even the great players, when they get older, are benched for younger guys. Don't take it personally."

"Yeah. True. I guess my company figured they could save some money by eliminating my salary. Can't blame 'em. It's business." Nick sighed. "Something'll break."

Naomi reached for Nick's hand and held it.

"Sure will, Nick. When one door closes, another opens somewhere else. Something good's coming your way. I feel it." Whitherspoon put his hand on Nick's shoulder. "Can I buy you another beer?"

"Is Elway a hall-of-fame quarterback?" Nick grinned.

"I'll take that as a yes."

The Broncos beat a tough Seattle Seahawks team with a touchdown drive in the final minutes of the game. To celebrate the hard-won victory, Whitherspoon took Naomi and Nick to dinner at his favorite area restaurant, Elway's. After ordering the special of the day, "Mile-High Surf and Turf," he toasted the couple. "I'm so glad you found each other. She's a good woman, Nick. Here's to a long and happy marriage." He touched their glasses.

Naomi turned and smiled at Nick. "I love you, dear. You've made me so happy."

"Love you, too," Nick answered. "And I'm the luckiest man in the world to have you."

Whitherspoon's vision blurred. He averted his eyes so they wouldn't see the tears forming. He didn't need to do that because at that moment Nick and Naomi didn't even know Whitherspoon existed, their eyes too busy focusing on each other.

The next day, as Whitherspoon waited for takeoff on his flight to Cody, he looked at his watch and saw he had a few minutes before the announcement to turn off cell phones. He called an old colleague, Christopher Wagner. "Wags, how're ya doing?"

"Kingpin! Can't complain."

"Great. Listen, I need a favor. There's a public relations executive I know. Name's Nick Dosh. I think he's a good fit for your company. Good man. Will you interview him?"

"Sure. We have an opening right now. Can you forward his contact information?"

"As soon as I get checked into my hotel in Cody."

"Good. We start interviewing next week."

"That's wonderful. Hey, don't tell him I set it up. Say hi to Patti. Gotta go. Thanks a million."

—⚏—

Whitherspoon checked into his hotel in Cody and e-mailed Nick Dosh's contact information to Wagner as promised. He drove around in his rental car to look at familiar places. *All I ever wanted when I came to Cody was a chance to prove myself, and they gave it to me. What happened?*

Whitherspoon had made a lot of friends in Cody as a cub reporter in his first full-time journalism job. Business owners and elected officials loved his stories promoting the city. He relished his role as a local celebrity, but his early success filled him with conceit, and he soon thought himself too big for a town the size of Cody. His boss at the time, Douglas Dale, picked another reporter over him for a juicy assignment to write a regular column with a byline. He met with Dale to find out why he wasn't given the promotion. Dale responded that Whitherspoon needed to develop a writing style with more of an edge and be more aggressive as a reporter.

After being bypassed for advancement, Whitherspoon changed. *They want aggressive and edgy? I'll give them aggressive and edgy. Besides, this one-horse town's only a stepping-stone anyway. Before long I'll be outta here, and I'll never look back.* He forgot about the many people who helped him along the way and even turned his back on former colleagues and friends. Whitherspoon eventually got a bigger job in Denver. He cut everyone from Cody out of his life and never looked back, except once: to write a hit piece, calling out the city's tourist attractions as scams.

Now, driving through Cody, these recollections troubled Whitherspoon. *I'll make it right. I'll get with people and apologize. I'll fix things.*

He drove to his old apartment and office. Then he cruised by the watering hole where he boasted he would someday star as the senior anchor of a news department. He went to the coffee shop he used to frequent and checked out every customer from head to toe, hoping to recognize an old friend or business contact. He didn't recognize anyone, and nobody recognized him.

After ordering a cheeseburger and fries, he pulled out a tattered address book from his lapel pocket, opened it up, and dialed a number. "Hello, is this Lance?"

"Yes. Speaking."

"Tom Whitherspoon here. I'm in town for a couple of days and wondered if you'd like to get together for a drink."

"Oh, hello. Nice hearing from you. Sorry, I have a lot to get done in the next few days."

"How's everything?"

"Fine. Hey, thanks for calling...ah...Tom. I gotta run."

Whitherspoon leafed through his address book, found several other numbers, and left messages. He decided to call his old boss at the newspaper. "May I speak with Mr. Dale?"

The receptionist answered. "He doesn't work here anymore."

He asked for three former coworkers. They didn't work there either. At last, he asked the receptionist if she had ever heard of Thomas Whitherspoon.

"Can't say that I have," she said.

Whitherspoon pressed his little address book flat with his fingertips so he could see a faint number. He punched it into his cell phone. "May I speak with Don Johnston? Tell him it's Tom Whitherspoon. I used to work with him."

"I'll check." After a few minutes on hold, the voice came back on the line. "Mr. Johnston's in a meeting now and expects it will last the rest of the day. Is there a message?"

"No message." He hung up.

Before his lunch arrived, Whitherspoon made a few more calls and left more messages. He read the local paper and reminisced at how it had changed since he worked there. It had a slicker look than when he wrote articles for it. He recognized a few names and businesses in the articles, while he ate his cheeseburger. He creased the paper and looked around the restaurant again. Still not seeing anyone he knew, he checked his cell phone. No one had returned his calls.

He watched people eating, astonished at how happy they looked. Whitherspoon recalled how all the servers in this diner used to know he liked apple pie à la mode for dessert. They just brought it; he didn't even have to ask. That memory made him smile.

A waitress interrupted his daydream. "Sir, would you like some dessert?"

Jolted from his reverie, he looked up at her. "Yes, please. I'd like apple pie à la mode."

"Sorry. We don't serve pie anymore. We do have a menu of healthy dessert snacks if you'd like to see it."

"No. That's all right. Check, please."

After paying the bill, he trudged into the fresh air and hiked down the long, winding street, examining the faces, looking into storefront windows, and dodging baby strollers. He pulled his cell phone from a front pocket to scan for messages. There were none. He checked the volume and then stuck the phone back in his pocket.

—⁂—

Whitherspoon thought the Buffalo Bill Historical Center was the number one attraction in Cody. Always his favorite, he had written many articles about the center and even won an award for a piece titled, "The Lifestyle of the Native Americans."

For the next three hours, Whitherspoon roamed through every exhibit, reading all the plaques and studying the museum pieces. His thoughts returned to the time when he had first discovered the center and had visited it often. After a few hours, his legs told him it was time to sit down somewhere, so he found a vacant bench and checked his phone for messages. There were none.

Now what am I going to do all evening? The Cody Rodeo. That's it. I'll go to the rodeo; it's on every night during the summer. Doors open at 7:00 p.m. I'm sure to see someone I know who'll remember me. If not, it'll keep me busy until I get some callbacks. When I get those, I'll schedule my meetings for tomorrow.

He bought himself a beer and a couple of hot dogs and walked down the aluminum bleachers to the front row so he could watch the cowboys in the staging area getting ready for their competitions. He had the row to himself except for a woman who looked about forty-five who sat at the opposite end draped in a worn, old-fashioned sweater inadequate for the unseasonably cold temperature. He placed his food on the adjoining bleacher seat and checked his cell phone for callbacks. Still none.

The public address system, loud and barely understandable, did little to enhance the visual spectacle and heart-stopping action of the rodeo competition. The sights, colors, and action overwhelmed the senses. The rodeo, a dramatic theater of danger, speed, and skill, played out for the fans as the competitors showed their mastery over horses, bulls, and calves while risking injury and death. Whitherspoon, surprised to see such a small crowd in attendance, cheered and clapped for the winners of each competition, men and women he had never heard of. Tonight, for a few hours at least, he was once again the young reporter from Cody, excited about his future. In one sense, he felt as if he'd never left, but things were different now, and so was he.

Two young boys in the cowboy prep area caught Whitherspoon's eye. One was about eleven years old and the other about seven. They appeared to be brothers. They organized their rodeo gear, putting on protective vests and tightening the straps. They tried on helmets and dug through their large sport bags, deciding which shirts to wear. The older boy dispensed advice to his brother, who nodded. They looked up at the woman and waved. She waved back. Whitherspoon then recognized that the woman in his row was their mother.

She kept one eye on her boys while she read a paperback, waiting for their competition. The gusting winds made the night even colder. She shivered and kept pulling her sweater tighter around her for warmth.

Whitherspoon walked to the woman's side of the row and sat down. "Your boys, huh?"

"Yeah." She placed her book face down on the bleachers so she wouldn't lose her place.

"I always wanted a couple of sons. But my ex-wife and I couldn't have children. Where did they get this passion for the rodeo?" Whitherspoon asked.

"I dunno. Their father was a bull rider, so maybe it's in their genes, but they don't know anything about him. He took off with another woman when they were still toddlers."

"Sorry. He didn't appreciate what a good woman he had."

Her eyes filled with tears.

"Do they come here every night?"

"Yep. Whenever there's a rodeo. When school's in session, they do their homework after we get home. As long as they keep up their studies, I'll keep bringing them here after I get off work."

"I've been here over an hour and they've been down in that pit, preparing the whole time."

"They're dedicated, that's for sure—bull riders, like their dad. We get here two hours early so they can prepare themselves physically and mentally. I read a book, sit on my cushion, and wait. We eat a lot of fast food." She grinned and brushed a strand of light brown hair from her freckled face.

Whitherspoon smiled in return and looked directly into her eyes for the first time and noticed they were blue. "Well, the wait's over. Boys' bull riding is next. I hope your sons do well."

"Thanks." Thinking their conversation over, she pulled her sweater tighter and turned back to watch the rodeo arena.

Whitherspoon zipped up his coat to keep out the frigid air. *This woman's shaking; she should wear a warmer coat.*

"Aren't you getting cold?" he asked. "I'm freezing."

She turned back to Whitherspoon. "A little. It is chilly for late August. With the fall coming, I will need to get a warm coat, but the boys come first. It's OK. I get paid next Friday, and if nothing comes up, I'll get a coat then."

The announcer's voice blasted in the overhead speakers. "Ladies and gentleman, the next event is boys' bull riding. Come on, cheer these young cowpokes—let's hear it."

Whitherspoon looked around and clapped along with about a hundred fans scattered around the mostly unoccupied bleachers. The younger brother competed first. His big brother leaned over the fence, barking last-minute instructions. Their mother got to her feet and yelled, "Come on, Duke, show 'em what you got."

The chute opened and the young bull bucked the boy off with his second hind leg kick. Little Duke landed hard on the ground, launching an explosion of dust. The people clapped and laughed at him. His mother yelled, "Good job, Duke! I'm proud of you."

Three more boys met the same fate—bucked off in seconds— then it was the older brother's turn. He looked up at his mom and waved. She rose up. "Come on, Tommy! You can do it, son!"

Little Duke, forearms leaning on the middle rail of the arena, shouted, "Show that bull who's boss, bro."

The chute opened and Tommy fell off backward within seconds. The night was over for the two brothers and their mom.

She watched in silence for a few tense seconds to make sure Tommy would get up off the ground. Once she knew he was OK, she yelled, "Good job, Tommy. Way to go."

"That was quick," Whitherspoon said.

"I thought they both did a great job."

"They did. I'm sorry. I didn't mean it like it came out. You guys going home?"

"Yeah. We leave when they're done. They get so down on themselves they won't want to talk. I'll take them out for a dessert on the way home—then homework and bed. Excuse me, I need to go congratulate them on their rides."

She leapfrogged down the bleachers to talk to them at the railing. Whitherspoon picked the book up off her purse and slipped in two one-hundred-dollar bills. He made his way up the aluminum steps to exit the grandstand. When he got to the top of the bleachers, he paused and checked his cell phone for messages. There were none.

Chapter 15

KINGPIN RETURNS

"Waddya think?" Leon Rump leaned over Fannie Larsen's computer.

She had just watched the demo Rump had made of her on-air work when she interned at Briggs News 20 the previous summer.

"I have to admit, Leon, it looks pretty good. That's what I had in mind. Now I have something to send out to TV stations when I apply for jobs."

"That's an excellent demo. I outdid myself on that one." He placed his hand on her shoulder.

Fannie extracted his hand off of her shoulder as if she was picking off a leech. Then she stood up. "You still have to get me a job."

"I got that covered. Kingpin's gonna help when he gets back."

"Good. I'm counting on you." She walked to the door of her dorm room and opened it. "OK, time to leave. I've got studying to do."

He closed it. "I expect a proper thank you."

She put her arms around him and kissed him. "How's that?"

"Pretty good for starters." He scooped her up in his arms, carried her to the bed, and laid her down, then started unbuttoning her blouse.

"Make it quick. I've got a test tomorrow."

—⚏—

The Picklers' home, filled with jubilant youth, seemed to bounce with excitement as Hannah Strollo and her teammates chattered enthusiastically about their season, favorite music, and boys. The mouthwatering smells of fresh pizza, salsa, and popcorn permeated the air, encouraging participants to gorge themselves on the array of chips, pretzels, and snacks strategically located within their reach. Music blared from their impressive sound system. The purpose of tonight's party, the launch of Project Hope, had brought together about forty teenagers eager to make a difference in their local community.

The Picklers, on opposite sides of the living room, were surrounded by young admirers. They had decided to put their personal trauma behind them by giving back to the people of Briggs Lake while he continued searching for a new job. They were living on their savings and a mysterious cashier's check for $20,000 that appeared in their mailbox one day. He had applied to teach journalism at the high school and to coach the girls' softball team since their coach retired at the end of the season. The coach recommended that Carl take his place since they had been friends for many years, and he respected Pickler's knowledge of the game and his athletic accomplishments at Arizona State. At one time they had even coached a Little League baseball team together.

"Could I have everyone's attention, please? Thank you." Carl moved to the center of the living room. "Thank you all for coming. Tonight we launch Project Hope to help those in our community with the greatest needs. Our first project is to raise money for the families of the slain taxi drivers, Manuel Dominguez and Chico Escobar."

The girls and some of their boyfriends erupted into cheers and applause to show their support for Project Hope and the victims' families. Hannah Strollo, team captain, spoke for all of them. "We're with you all the way, Mr. Pickler!"

"Thanks, Hannah. Marlene and I appreciate the commitment you and everyone else are willing to make for the success of this endeavor. We'd like everyone to put your name on at least one project at the table in the kitchen. You can sign up for the carwash, fashion show, or the landscaping day. We'll also play a few exhibition games against the Briggs Lake firefighter team. We'll raise some serious money for the Dominguez and Escobar families, and we'll have fun in the process, so let's get this party started."

The room seemed to shake when everyone clapped and yelled. Carl clapped his hands and danced through the room high-fiving everyone in his path.

Marlene studied her husband with a deep sense of respect. *That's the man I married: a strong, confident leader. He's back.* She caught his eye and gave him a big smile and a wave.

He smiled and blew her a kiss. He knew what she was thinking.

—⚬—

The next day Erin O'Haven made good on her offer to show Rex Martin around town. Their tour ended with a hike around Lakeside Park. It was a sunny day, something she was quick to point out that she had predicted on her previous newscast.

"You're a meteorological genius, Erin. What can I say?"

"Exactly, my boy. I'm glad you appreciate brilliance when it's staring you in the face. This walking path is one of my favorite places. It's such a peaceful and serene area. Good for your cardio too, Rex. You need more than weight lifting to keep fit. Don't forget the cardio." *Oh my God. He's such a hunk.*

"Yes, ma'am. I know the need for cardio. I do treadmill and elliptical machines. I'd like to get you in the weight room sometime."

I'm sure he'd like to get me in his bedroom too. She laughed. "Yeah, anytime. Why? Do you think my body needs toning up?"

Rex beamed. "Your body appears quite firm. I don't see any problems there. Weight training could help your stamina in holding up that pointer when you're doing weather."

He keeps checking me out, and I'm looking so-o-o fine. "Anytime, Rex. I love working out. Were you born in New Mexico?"

"No. Houston, Texas. Lived there most of my childhood. What about you?"

This dude is so into me, he can't take his eyes off me. "Minnesota, born and raised."

"Lots of Scandinavians there. You're Irish. How'd that work out?"

"Oh, there are plenty of Irishmen in Minnesota. Don't let those Ole and Lena jokes make you think we ever take a backseat to the Swedes, Norwegians, and Danes."

"You must get in lots of fights with them," Martin said.

"Not at all. Minnesotans don't fight each other."

He made a face. "I don't believe you. Everyone fights."

"Haven't you ever heard of 'Minnesota Nice'?"

"What's that?"

"The people of Minnesota are courteous, low-key, and mild-mannered."

"Sounds like 'passive-aggressive' to me." Martin smiled.

Erin laughed. "Yeah. We're that too."

They stopped walking when they saw a coyote about a hundred yards away. It glared at them for a few seconds then trotted out of sight to some scrub bushes.

"They're not afraid of anything, are they?" he said. "Fearless is the only way to be."

"For sure. They're real survivors. They've learned to adapt. People around here aren't supposed to feed them in town, but they sometimes rob garbage cans. You'll notice there are no feral cats in Briggs Lake. Can you guess why?"

"They ought to hunt them down and kill them," Martin said as they resumed walking.

"They tried about ten years ago, and then we had an epidemic of rabbits that ate every green thing in sight—ravaging everyone's garden and landscaping. After the coyotes were eliminated, rabbits had no predators to keep their population down. Now shooting coyotes within five miles of the city limits is banned, unless they are attacking you or your dog."

Rex picked up the pace. "Hey, Queen of Cardio, if we go faster we'll get more cardio work in."

"Yeah. Then we'll miss the pageantry and splendor of the park," Erin said, maintaining the slower pace. "Life's full of trade-offs, my boy."

"True. Speaking of nationalities, Ronnie Gaboni's gotta be an Italian. What about Kingpin and Carol?"

"Don't know. They never talk about their heritage." She bent over to take a drink at a water fountain. *I'm sure he's checking out my ass. Take a good look, buddy.*

When she raised up, she asked, "What about you?"

"What do you think I am?"

"Please tell me you're Irish. My parents would have a meltdown if they knew I wasn't hanging around my people."

Martin laughed and lowered his mouth to the fountain for a drink. When he finished, he wiped his mouth on the upper arm of his t-shirt. Pointing at a man playing catch with his son, he said, "Look at that."

He stopped walking to study a man who was teaching his son the proper technique for throwing a baseball, while Erin took the opportunity to snap a couple of pictures of the mountains and upload them to her Facebook page.

Erin, preoccupied with her photography, didn't see a rattle-snake she had nearly stepped on. The startled diamondback began making a rattling sound and coiled to strike her. Rex, alert to the situation, found a big rock and slammed it down on the snake's head, crushing it. The body continued to coil and wriggle, so he picked up another large stone and finished it off.

"That sucker won't bother us anymore," he said.

"Oh, Rex, you saved my life." She ran over and hugged him. "Thank you, thank you thank you. You're my hero."

—⚏—

Whitherspoon scanned his renovated office and smiled. It had everything he wanted. His money shot, taken when he became senior anchor, hung in a prominent spot for all to see. His private restroom and makeup area, with a full-length mirror, glistened under white ceiling lights. He believed the recessed lighting he had fought so hard for would soften age lines and give him a more youthful appearance when he received visitors. He loved the spectacular view from his windows and could imagine himself strategizing his next career move while looking at the traffic below. The office was everything he wanted it to be, except for one thing. He had to share it with Rex Martin.

"You like it, Kingpin?" Martin asked, breaking the silence.

"I like it. Looks good." Gesturing toward the main wall, he asked, "Did you notice my head shot?"

"Yes I did, and it looks great."

"Well, listen. That's my favorite picture. I call it my money shot. It must never be askew. Keep an eye on it. If you see it tilted, straighten it up."

"Sure. You look so young in that picture."

"Thanks. I agree."

Martin wanted to change the subject. "I appreciate you letting me share the office."

Like I had a choice. "No problem."

"I'm sure you've noticed that one desk is bigger and more prominent. That's yours."

"I hadn't noticed."

"Yeah, I insisted. 'That one's gotta be for the Kingpin,' I said."

Big deal. "Thanks." With a quick nod to Martin, Whitherspoon placed his business planner on the bigger desk to stake his claim.

Leon Rump barged in. "Welcome back, Kingpin. How d'ya like it?"

"Looks good." Whirling from Rump to Martin, he asked, "Could you excuse me and your uncle for fifteen minutes?"

"Sure. Take your time. I've got to visit Detective Strollo anyway," Martin said.

Whitherspoon remembered that Martin and had been covering the murder investigations for the station. "How's it going?"

"Slow. I sure wish Strollo would loosen up with some news I
can share tonight on the show. He's tight-lipped. See you later."
Martin scooted out of the office carrying a portfolio.

Whitherspoon took off his coat, placed it over his desk chair,
and loosened his tie. "Good to see you, Leon. Did you get Fannie's
demo reel done?"

"Yeah. She loved it, but she won't be satisfied until we get her
a job. I told her when you got back you'd get right on it." Leon
helped himself to a chair near Whitherspoon's desk.

Whitherspoon sat down behind his desk for the first time,
rocking to test the springs of the chair before looking at Rump.
"I've been doing a lot of thinking about Fannie. I feel like she's
blackmailing us. I don't mind helping her get some interviews,
but I don't like her threats."

"Don't forget—Fannie's eyewitness testimony against Pickler
convinced Jocko to let him go."

"And it helped you get your nephew a job," Whitherspoon
added.

"I know—good for both of us. It took the pressure off you.
Pickler wanted your job, to be the Kingpin. Rex is different. He's
got your back."

"But here's the thing, Leon—we can't guarantee Fannie a job."

"Well, think about this—if we don't get her a job, she'll go to
Samantha and we'll lose ours."

"Look, you're the one who made the promises to her, not me.
Excuse me, I have work to do." Whitherspoon dismissed Rump
with a wave of his hand and reached for a stack of Nielsen ratings.

—⁂—

After organizing his desk, Whitherspoon took some time to
reflect on the situation. He strummed his fingers on the new desk
while looking at a TV mounted on the wall tuned to Briggs News

20. Three TVs on an adjacent wall were tuned to his competitors so he could monitor their newscasts.

Fannie's a problem. She's irrational if she expects us to guarantee her a job. Leon said he told her that, but did he?

I could go to Samantha and tell her everything myself. That would eliminate the leverage Fannie has over us, and it would clear Pickler's name. Then Leon and I get fired. With me out of the picture, Rex becomes the senior anchor: the Kingpin. He's the big winner in all this. But what happens to me? I'm walking the streets, job hunting at age sixty. Who'd hire me?

She could be bluffing. If I keep my mouth shut, I keep my job. Then I can use my position in the media to help others, even Pickler someday. He's a good man. He'll land on his feet.

Whitherspoon's thoughts were interrupted when Carol Lackey paraded into his office. Her hair evidenced a recent trip to the beauty shop, and she wore a brand-new gray flannel business suit and black pumps. She brought a silent companion: the overpowering smell of cologne.

"Welcome back, Tom! We all missed you around here." She put her arms around him.

"I missed everyone too. Especially you, Carol. I had no one to insult me, and no one does it as well as you."

"Practice makes perfect. Somebody's gotta do it. D'ya think it's easy keeping an egomaniac like you humble?"

"It's gotta be the hardest job in the world."

"Couldn't have said it better myself. How was Denver?"

"Saw my ex and her new husband. We went to a Broncos preseason game and then to dinner. They're a happy couple. Leaving me was the best decision she ever made."

"Yeah, Naomi's got to be real happy she cut you loose." She smiled. "Smart girl."

"Can't argue with that." Whitherspoon chuckled.

"I have something to give you and something to ask you. Excuse me. I'll be right back." She darted out into the hallway and vaulted back carrying a large bag. "After you open this up, I need to ask you a question. Go ahead, open it up." Carol observed him with the intensity of a basketball coach watching her players in a big game. "What're you waiting for?"

"You're so damn pushy, Carol. Don't worry. I'll open it up." Whitherspoon unwrapped the box, folding up the layers of paper to save them. Removing the last sheet of paper revealed a beautiful leather attaché case. The metal plate under the handle bore his initials, T.O.W., for Thomas Osborne Whitherspoon.

"What do you think?"

"It's awesome. Thank you so much." He set the case down and embraced her.

After a few seconds, she pushed him away. "Now open it."

He slid open the double latches and lifted up the top, revealing two tickets to the local community theater production of *Romeo and Juliet*.

"Oh, Carol, you shouldn't have done all this. Now you're making me feel guilty for how I've treated you through the years."

"Good. My plan is working." She laughed. "Here's the deal—I'll let you make it up to me by taking me to *Romeo and Juliet*."

"Don't you see enough of me at work?"

"I bought these tickets for a cancer fund-raiser. I'm sacrificing myself for a good cause."

"When?"

"This Saturday."

"It's a date. Now get outta here. I have work to do."

"Since when do you do any work?" She waved and left in triumph with a wide smile.

A few minutes later his cell phone rang.

"Whitherspoon."

"Hi, Tom. It's Carmaletta. The boys got your letter about the rodeo in Wyoming and the postcard of the Broncos team picture. They were thrilled. Thanks a lot. They love football, but they're Arizona Cardinal Fans."

"I guess I'll have to convert them. How are they doing?"

She paused, then spoke, emphasizing every word, "Oh, they're doing great. They're big fans of yours too and keep telling stories about the night they spent with you at the softball game."

"Well, I've sure got them fooled, don't I, Carmaletta?"

"You sure do. Say, I'm calling to invite you to dinner. I'm a pretty good cook, if I do say so myself. The boys say you like a good T-bone steak. We've got a free night and would like to repay your kindness to us. I'll even brew some of my special coffee just for you."

"Your coffee? That's an offer I can't refuse. When?"

"This Saturday."

"Oh no! I'm so sorry. I have another commitment. I have a lot of catching up to do. Can I get back with you and give you some dates when I'm free?"

She paused before answering in a quiet tone. "Sure. Let me know."

"Deal. Sorry it didn't work out this time."

"I understand. I know you're a very busy man, but I thought I'd give it a try and—"

"Hey, tell the boys I said hi. We'll talk soon." He hung up, bowed his head, closed his eyes, and took a deep breath, which he exhaled very slowly.

—◆—

"OK, quiet on the set...counting down to show...Three...two... one...go."

"Good evening, this is Rex Martin. Briggs News 20 starts now. I'm pleased to announce the return of our senior anchor, Thomas Whitherspoon. Welcome back, Tom!"

"Thanks, Rex! It's good to be back. Now for tonight's news..."

The newscast continued as usual with Erin's weather report and Ronnie's sports update. The show moved along at a quick pace. Whitherspoon and Martin tossed to each other as they alternated news reports. Martin had upped his game since coming on board, and Whitherspoon performed as if he had never left.

When the newscast ended, the floor director disconnected Martin and Whitherspoon from their microphones. "How'd it feel, Kingpin?"

"Amazing. What a high. I love working the anchor's desk. I was born to do this job," said an elated Whitherspoon.

Whitherspoon noticed the crew didn't share his excitement to be back on the newscast. They weren't rude or hostile, but he expected more of a response after a two-month absence. "How'd I do?"

The crew ignored the question, choosing instead to stow the equipment and prepare the studio for the next newscast.

After an embarrassing silence, the floor director volunteered, "Looked good to us, Kingpin."

"Hey, would anyone like to go out for a beer after the second newscast?"

Silence was the only answer. There were no takers.

The awkwardness broke when Martin, who had been speaking with Ronnie and Erin, spoke up. "I'll take you up on the offer, Kingpin. You said you were buying, right?"

"I didn't say that, Rex, but I'll buy. Next time it's on you, though, since you're doing so well in your new job," Whitherspoon joked.

The crew ignored the exchange.

—⁂—

After the last newscast, Whitherspoon and Martin went out for a beer. Whitherspoon craned to check for familiar faces in Hoochy's dining room as they were led to a table, but he didn't see anyone he knew. No one recognized him except the hostess.

"Good evening, Mr. Whitherspoon," she said.

"Is Trixie-Lee working tonight?"

"Yes, she is."

"I want her to wait on us."

"No problem. I'll get her."

It didn't take long for Trixie-Lee to gallop out of the kitchen, her long braid bouncing disobediently on her back as she walked. After plucking the contents of her tray and placing them on an adjoining table, she glanced at Whitherspoon. Her eyes brightened as she approached. Stopping at their table, she let the hand holding the empty tray fall to her side. "Mr. Kingpin! How are you this evening?"

"Fine. Miss me?"

"Did you go somewhere?" She giggled.

"Oh, never mind." Whitherspoon made a face showing mocked disgust. "It's good to see you. Still keeping it real?"

"Sure."

"Are you staying out of trouble?"

"Of course not."

"Good. A couple of beers, please. Coors Light." After saying this, Whitherspoon looked at Martin, who nodded in confirmation. "Keep a close eye on us for refills in case we run low on our medication. You must've met my new partner by now, Rex Martin. Don't let the short hair scare you."

"Hello, Trixie-Lee," Martin nodded.

"Hi, Mr. Martin. I think I've seen you in here before. I'll get your beers."

A few minutes later, she returned with their drinks. Before leaving, she said, "Let me know if you need anything."

Martin updated Whitherspoon on the happenings of Briggs News 20 during his absence. He shared ideas he and Jocko had discussed to attract younger viewers to the newscast. "We're talking about eliminating the anchor desk."

"Eliminating the anchor desk?" Whitherspoon exhaled with a whistle. "Kind of radical, isn't it? Seriously?"

"Yes. They're so old-fashioned. We should be standing in the middle of the newsroom with TV monitors and producers working at their desks in the background."

Whitherspoon took a big mouthful and swallowed hard. "Interesting. What other changes have you been discussing?"

"Jocko and I think we should ask viewers to comment on stories on Facebook and Twitter. Using social media outlets is another good way to build a youthful fan base. Younger viewers like to express their opinions and comments on their smartphones. We want to set up chat rooms and let them rate and comment on our stories and even choose topics."

Whitherspoon felt a bit dizzy. "I could use a 'smartphone for dummies.' I'm all thumbs on a computer. I can't imagine how they can even type on them, let alone read from them. I did get an iPhone, but I still don't know how to use it. Guess I should take a course." He looked at Martin and shrugged. "Don't you think Twitter, Facebook, and other social media are just temporary fads anyway?"

"No. They're here to stay, Kingpin. Young people today don't want to listen to the news. They want to connect and interact—they like two-way communication." He took a swig of beer. "We need to aim our programming at the 18-24 demographics. They're gold for our advertising clients. They love to spend money."

Now this punk thinks he can lecture me on demographics and the ad sales game. "Don't get ahead of yourself. If Jocko's not behind your ideas, they're not going anywhere."

"He's committed to these ideas."

"Really?"

"In fact, next week he's asked me to launch a Briggs News 20 website, Facebook, and Twitter accounts. I volunteered to set them up and to monitor them until we can find a permanent administrator. Young people want to connect with us—they're not passive listeners."

"Wonderful, Rex. Good for you. Yeah, you're right. Come to think of it, our core audience has gotten older." The conversation made Whitherspoon feel old. He looked around the room, thinking of a way to change the subject. "How's 'The Good News Show' doing?"

"Coming along fine. Carol's helped me a lot to put the show together. She responds to the calls and e-mails and helps select the charity we'll highlight on each week's show."

Whitherspoon nodded. "She's a piece of work."

"Sure is. And she thinks the world of you. I'll be right back." Martin got up to use the restroom.

Seeing Whitherspoon alone, Trixie-Lee took the opportunity to come to the table. "I heard you had a health issue. You OK?"

"I'm fine. How're your college classes going?"

"Good."

"Stay with it. You're too smart to work as a waitress all your life."

"Thanks for saying that. I do want to finish and go into teaching."

"Say, I wanna tell you, I'm sorry for all the times I flirted with you and used sexual innuendo. I thought I was being funny and witty. Now I realize I was just being a disrespectful asshole."

Trixie-Lee leaned in and put her arm around him. "It's OK. I knew how you meant it. Deep down, I've always felt you were a good man."

"I'm not. I've done some very bad things to some very good people."

Martin returned. After sitting down and moving his chair forward, he gestured toward Trixie-Lee, now flitting across the dining room at full speed. "She looks Mexican."

"I've never asked," Whitherspoon said.

"Dark skin and black hair. Gotta be a Mexican."

"She's a cool lady, Rex. That's all I know." He sipped his Coors Light. "How's your Uncle Leon?"

"Doing well. Working on an assignment in Tempe that's taken a lot of his time."

Whitherspoon nodded. *He must have been helping Fannie with that demo reel. That reminds me—I need to get her some referrals tomorrow. I hope Rump is keeping her happy.*

"The crew seemed kind of down tonight. What's going on with them?" Whitherspoon fixed his gaze on Martin.

"I haven't noticed anything. They've seemed OK to me. What do you mean?"

"Oh, I don't know. Maybe it's just me. They're all so young—sometimes I feel old."

"Tom, have you ever thought about retiring?" Martin leaned over the table. "You're getting up there, and who needs the stress? You don't have anything to prove. You've had a great career. Turn the page—take care of your health."

"My health is fine, Rex, and I'm too young to retire. Why is everyone worrying about my health? I was born to do the evening news, and I'm at the top of my game." He leaned back in his chair and smiled. "But thanks for your concern." *He'd love having me out of the way.*

"I just brought it up because you said sometimes you feel old."

"I said 'sometimes.' Not all the time. Most of the time I feel great. My time off has recharged my batteries. I feel great right now."

"Just a suggestion. Thanks for the beers. I gotta go." Martin pushed his chair back and got up. "See you tomorrow."

Grabbing the check, Whitherspoon replied, "Thanks for the company, Rex. You're doing great on the show, by the way."

"Thanks. Welcome back."

Martin walked out of Hoochy's.

While Whitherspoon waited at the cash register for the hostess to ring up his check, Trixie-Lee came to his side and softly punched his arm. "Thank you for encouraging me to finish school."

Chapter 16

CARMALETTA'S MIRACLE

Later that week, Whitherspoon met with the city manager, Biff McCoy.

"Let me get this straight. You're willing to put up a million dollars to build a shelter for abused women. You don't want it named after you, and you don't want anyone to know you gave the gift. Hiring Carmaletta Dominguez is the only thing you're asking in return."

"Correct." Whitherspoon nodded.

"But, why?"

"That's my business. I'll also fund the first year of its operation if you can get the mayor and council to make it a permanent line item in the budget going forward."

McCoy's perplexed look changed into a smile. "I think I can make that happen."

"Good. Then we have a deal?"

"Tentatively, yes. I'm just the city manager. I have to lay out your terms to the mayor and council to make sure they're in agreement and willing to make the long-term investment. I'll suggest we move funding from other social budget items to cover the operating expenses after the first year. I don't think they'll have a problem. We've discussed running a battered women's shelter for a long time."

"Excellent." Whitherspoon got up to leave. "Let me know when it's a done deal, and I'll do an electronic funds transfer."

"Thanks, Mr. Whitherspoon—really generous of you. I don't know what to say."

"You don't have to say anything. Just keep my identity private and hire Mrs. Dominguez." He saluted the city manager with a wave, turned on his heel in a crisp military fashion, and marched out of the office.

The city manager stroked the stubble on his chin and shook his head. *Holy shit.*

—⚏—

Once in his Porsche, Whitherspoon speed-dialed Carmaletta. "Hello?"

"Hi, Carmaletta. Tom. Can I take you up on the standing offer for some of your great coffee?"

"Good to hear your voice. When are you coming over?"

"I'm across town and have to get some gas first. How about an hour from now?"

"Great. See you then."

After gassing his Porsche, Whitherspoon felt sharp pains in his chest and stomach. He worried that a serious illness had infected him. Part of him wanted to go to a doctor and get checked out. Whitherspoon concluded a doctor might hospitalize him for observation and tests. If that happened, Jocko would find out and use the hospitalization as an excuse to reorganize him out of the news department. He couldn't afford to take that chance, so he would tough it out. Reaching into the glove compartment, he found a bottle of Tums and swallowed a handful, hoping for the best.

When he arrived at Carmaletta's home, she gave him a big squeeze. Whitherspoon felt warm all over, and the chest and stomach pains immediately went away. The large weight had been lifted off his shoulders, and he smelled the fragrance of lilacs from her perfume. His brow smoothed and his facial muscles relaxed, except for those creating an ever-widening smile.

"You sure know how to make a person feel welcome," he said.

"We missed you." She took him by the arm and guided him to a steaming-hot cup of coffee on the kitchen table. The coffee filled the room with its rich aroma.

"Don't mind if I do." He eased into a chair and tasted the coffee. "Hits the spot. You sure know how to make a good cup of coffee. Thanks so much."

"Can I get you a Danish?"

"No thanks, just coffee. How're the boys?"

"They're doing great. They love school and have good teachers this year." She went into the kitchen and retrieved two sealed envelopes. "They wrote notes to thank you for taking them to the game. I've been meaning to mail them to you." She handed them to him. "Open them up later so we can use this time to talk."

"Can't wait to read them. Say, does your church believe in faith healing?"

She picked up her own cup of coffee from the counter and sat in a chair opposite him. "We sure do. We pray for healing all the time. Why?"

Whitherspoon blurted out, "Don't tell anyone. I've had some chest and stomach pain, and I'm a little concerned it could be something serious. The pains stopped immediately when you touched me. But I'm afraid they'll come back."

"You look healthy to me. By the way, I've already been praying for you."

"Good. Keep it up. I need it."

"We all do. You're really a kind and generous man."

He choked up. "Believe me, I've got a lot of issues."

"Who doesn't?"

"I'm sorry. Here you've lost your husband, and I'm sitting in your kitchen whining about a stomachache."

"I don't mind."

"Do you believe in angels?" he asked.

"Sure."

"One's talking to me—an angel, I mean. At least I think he is, but he hasn't said that in so many words. Only he doesn't have wings. He dresses like a volunteer at the hospital, and he has other disguises. He says giving is its own reward. He's giving me a second chance to change my ways. It's just that I'm afraid it's too late to change."

Carmaletta reached both hands across the table and put them on top of his, rubbing and holding them. "It's never too late."

Those words and the tender touch triggered an avalanche of tears he could not control. "I hope you're right."

"Undoing the damage is another thing," she said softly, still holding his hands. "You can't change the past, but you can change yourself."

"I've done a bunch of bad things to hurt an innocent family. I want to come clean—fess up to what I did—but I'm afraid I'll lose my job and everything I've worked for all these years."

"You'll never have peace of mind until you get honest with what you've done. If you tell the truth, you can always look yourself in the mirror."

"That's never been a problem for me." Whitherspoon chuckled. "I've always enjoyed looking at myself in the mirror—except it's for all the wrong reasons."

She laughed. "You're too funny."

"I've been called a lot of things—never funny." He had a mischievous gleam in his eyes. "I hope you mean 'funny' funny and not 'weird' funny."

"I mean you're funny *and* you're weird." She giggled.

"Thanks for the coffee and good advice. I'm feeling wonderful. Time to go to work and earn my keep."

"Thanks for stopping by. I'll tell the boys you said hi. They'll want to see you, too, you know." She swung open the refrigerator and removed a large paper bag. "I made you a lunch. There's a ham and cheese sandwich, a salad, and a couple of my homemade chocolate chip cookies."

"Thanks. You didn't need to feed me."

"I wanted to." She walked him to the front door and handed him the bag. "There's also a letter in there from me. You can read it when you're eating your lunch."

"Very sweet of you, Carmaletta. I'll be in touch." He noticed her shoulder-length curly brown hair for the first time. *This woman has beautiful hair.* Then he bounded down the stairs with his lunch and letters in hand.

She stood in the doorway until he drove out of view.

—⚬—

Later in the day, when he took a break for lunch, he got a Diet Coke from the vending machine in the break room. Whitherspoon knew he could have some privacy in the office, since Martin had scheduled some interviews at a local school. After wolfing down the ham sandwich and salad, he read the notes from Jason and Jamie, saving Carmaletta's for last.

Dear Tom,

This has been the worst five months of my life. I lost the man I've loved since my youth. My future is uncertain. I don't know what will happen to us. But I trust in the good Lord to see me through, He sent you to me to remind me there are good people out there who care and who are looking out for me and the boys. And you have given my sons something I could not, the companionship of a man who is a role model. Thank you from the bottom of my heart.

With kindest regards,

Carmaletta Dominguez

He set the note on his desk, leaned back in his chair, and closed his eyes.

Dear God, if you're up there, tell me what to do about Fannie Larsen, and I don't know how to make things right with Pickler. Help me. Thanks.

Rump rushed in. "Hey, Kingpin, got a minute?"

"Sure."

"I got a call from Fannie Larsen. She thinks she's getting a job. She's up for a second interview."

"Where? Was it one of the contacts gave her?"

"No. Someplace in Colorado. Never heard of it. She'll be a general assignment reporter and a substitute for the weekend anchor. She's ecstatic. Said she couldn't thank me enough." He chuckled.

"Yeah. And I'm sure you gave her some suggestions."

Rump cracked up. "I have no idea what you're talking about," he said and made a gesture that feigned complete ignorance of the comment's meaning.

"We're off the hook now. This is great news." Whitherspoon jumped from his chair, and they fist-bumped each other.

"It looks like we did it," Rump said.

"We sure did." Whitherspoon glowed. "We sure did."

Seeing the chocolate chip cookies Carmaletta made sitting on a white napkin on the desk, Rump pointed to them. "Are you going to eat those?"

"As a matter of fact, I am."

Chapter 17

PROJECT HOPE

The row of cars began at the back parking lot of the food mart and extended around the block. Two teenage girls, in matching orange bikinis, held signs: Free Car Wash for Donations. The line moved fast, and the cars emerged sparkling clean as the stack of cash donations mounted in an ever-increasing heap.

Carl led the washing crew that soaped the cars using gigantic sponges, and Marlene's team followed by using several garden hoses to rinse them. Hannah Strollo guided the drivers to an open area in the parking lot where a dozen swimsuit-clad girls descended on the vehicles, wiping them dry with long white rags. Two girls sprayed Armor All on the tires, and a couple polished the chrome as the finishing touch of the process before the drivers exited to the friendly waves of the appreciative volunteers.

While their cars were getting the once-over, the customers received explanations from the girls how donations were going to help the families of the dead cab drivers. Wallets opened up and customers tossed fists of cash into the donation bucket.

After six hours of nonstop car washing, things quieted down. "So how're we doing, girls?" Pickler asked.

The girl holding the donation bucket announced, "We have eight hundred dollars so far, Mr. Pickler."

"OK. Let's keep pushing until we make a thousand. We can do it." When a car came into the washing area, Carl jumped to his feet, revealing a rag dangling from his back pocket. Marlene couldn't resist the temptation. She turned on the hose and trained a tight stream at the back of her husband's head, which knocked his baseball cap off. He turned to see who had squirted him, and when he figured out it was Marlene, he pointed his finger at her. "You'll pay for this!"

"Sorry, buddy. You're not fast enough to catch the blond bomber!"

"We'll see, young lady. We'll see. Keep your mind on your work. You know I'm a hard guy to keep up with once I get rolling."

She shot another burst at his head, and he ducked.

"I'm warning you, hosing person, you're pressing your luck over there."

The girls on Marlene's team giggled at her antics while those on Carl's team looked the other way so he wouldn't see them laughing.

By the end of the day, they had reached their goal of one thousand dollars in contributions. He gathered everyone around him. "Thank you all for the great job. Not only are you excellent softball players, you're a fantastic team."

"You've made us a better team than we were," Hannah said, holding up a manila envelope. "Which brings me to this." She opened the envelope and took out a letter. "This is a letter from all the girls on the softball team—everyone signed it—asking the school board to hire you as a teacher and our new softball coach."

The girls surrounded Pickler, clapping.

"I don't know what to say, but thanks a lot."

A camera crew from Briggs News 20 showed up and interviewed the team and the Picklers. Project Hope was chosen as a weekly winner in "The Good News Show."

Chapter 18

CARMALETTA GETS A JOB

September passed quickly for Whitherspoon. "The Good News Show" continued to garner solid ratings, and he poured his energies into his work as never before, researching stories and rewriting scripts until they were honed to perfection. Whitherspoon called Carmaletta every day to check on her and the boys. The calls began and ended with the boys; in between, they talked about themselves, sharing their hopes and dreams and trivial day-to-day occurrences. On the weekends, he took Jamie and Jason to football games, action movies, and to the park to play catch.

One day, as Carmaletta unpacked groceries on her kitchen counter, the phone rang.

"This is she. How may I help you?"

"Mrs. Dominguez, this is Biff McCoy. I'm the city manager of Briggs Lake. You applied a few weeks ago for an opening we had in our accounting department, but I think you're also qualified for another opportunity. I see you had an extensive business background before becoming a stay-at-home mom, and your references were outstanding. I would like to offer you a job working for the city, running a women's shelter."

"Oh, I'd love to do it," she said. "What kind of schedule? I've got two young sons."

"We'll need you for some weekend and evening events, but we'll work with you on the schedule so your family doesn't suffer. How does that sound?"

"It sounds great."

"We'll discuss salary when the HR department finishes determining the wage structure. I'm pretty sure you'll be quite satisfied—from what I've seen of the preliminary numbers, the position pays much more than the accounting job. Plus, you'll get annual raises and the city's medical and dental plans. We even offer a matching 401(k) program."

"Exactly what I need!" She felt her face getting hot and tears forming. She fanned her face with her free hand. "Thank you so much."

"OK. We'll get HR going on the paperwork, and when they're done with the wage survey I'll call you back. We'll meet here and go over all the details. If the terms look good, you can sign the work contract at that time."

"Thank you." She sniffed, tears running down both cheeks. "God bless you, sir."

When the call ended, she sat at her kitchen table, put her head in her hands, and wept.

Chapter 19

KINGPIN'S LIFE CHANGES AGAIN

On Friday, Whitherspoon got a call from Jocko asking him to come to his office. He arrived to find the door closed, so he knocked.

"Come on in," Jocko's voice blasted from the other side of the door.

Whitherspoon opened the door a crack and peered in. "You wanted to see me, Jocko?"

"Yes, Tom. Please come in." Jocko, standing by the window, coffee mug in his left hand, motioned toward an empty chair at his conference table. "Samantha and I need to speak with you for a few minutes."

Whitherspoon spotted Samantha sitting in the corner of the room and nodded. "Hello, Samantha."

"Hello, Tom," she said.

Jocko shuffled to his office door, closing it before sitting at the table with Whitherspoon. "Tom, I'm not sure how to say this in the best way, so I'm just going to say it. Briggs News 20 has decided not to renew your contract when the term is up. You've done a marvelous job for us, but the board of directors has decided to go in a different direction."

"You're kidding, right?" Whitherspoon looked at Samantha and then back at Jocko. "After all I've done for you, Jocko? This is what I get?"

Jocko looked down and took a deep breath. "You've had a good run here, yes, and we appreciate all you've done to build our news department and its ratings, but management feels it's time for a change."

"You *are* management, Jocko!"

"Yes, but remember, I answer to a board of directors."

"Why didn't you fight for me? Why didn't you tell them how valuable I am? I don't get it. The ratings and revenues are solid." Whitherspoon held up his hands, palms up, fingers spread apart. "Don't those things mean anything anymore?"

"Sure. But there are other considerations. We're planning for the future and need to develop the next generation of on-air talent. I think it's best for the station to do it now, and probably for you too. Maybe this is a good time for you to take it easy—focus on your health."

"My health is fine, Jocko. I've told you that over and over. Why is everyone so damn worried about my health? Do you want calls or letters from my doctors? What?"

"Why not take this opportunity to retire and enjoy life?" Jocko said.

"Reporting the news in prime time *is* my life. Don't you get that?"

Samantha stopped taking notes and leaned toward Whitherspoon. "Tom, if you would prefer to leave the station right away, we're prepared to pay out your contract."

"Aren't you listening to what I'm saying? I don't want to leave. I don't want to retire. My health is fine. I want to keep working—I'm the Kingpin. I'm pulling in the numbers for you. What's the problem?" He continued shaking his head back and forth. "I can't believe this."

Jocko raised his hand. "Hear me out. We'd like to send you out in style. We'll produce a retrospective of your career, a video biography, about an hour in length, featuring clips from your on-air work. We'll do a first-rate job on it and commit all the resources necessary. You'll love it."

"Don't bother, Jocko. Seems like a lot of trouble for someone you're kicking down the road."

"No one's kicking you down the road. You know the transitory nature of our business as well as anyone. Like I said before, you've had a good run here."

"You're underestimating me and what I bring to the station."

"No, Tom. We appreciate your value and what you've done to develop our audience and ratings."

Whitherspoon pointed his finger at Jocko. "Let's face facts. You're not renewing my contract because of my age. I have an age-discrimination lawsuit, and if you think I won't go to court to protect my interests, you're wrong."

Jocko lowered his voice. "Your age has nothing to do with it."

"Oh, really? Nothing to do with it? At my age starting over at another station is impossible. I'll have to take you to court."

Jocko rubbed the top of his head. "I wouldn't do it if I were you. Win or lose, you'll never work in this industry again—you'll be a pariah."

"Maybe. But I'll ruin the reputation of this TV station, and my fans will turn on you."

Jocko glanced at Samantha.

Samantha put her pen down on the pad. "Tom, there's one other thing. It's come to our attention you made inappropriate comments to Stephanie, the photographer's assistant."

"Where'd you hear that?"

"Never mind. There were witnesses. If you choose the legal route, we'll depose her and terminate you for violating our sexual harassment policy." Samantha set her palms on the desktop. "So think long and hard before doing anything you'll regret."

Whitherspoon stared at the floor. *Rex must have said something. Backstabber—out for my job all along. That SOB.*

He looked back up at Jocko. "Yeah, OK. Anything else?"

"No. Let's get together after the weekend, on Monday, and talk more about the special on your career and how we can implement a smooth transition."

"Who'll take my place? Rex?"

"We don't know. We'll do a search and see what we come up with," Jocko said.

"Yeah, right. You've planned to replace me with him all along, haven't you?" He caught Samantha's eye.

She gave him a steady gaze. "Tom, this is a business decision and has nothing to do with your age or your health."

Whitherspoon took a deep breath and exhaled. "I gotta do what I gotta do. See you Monday."

Jocko nodded.

Whitherspoon stormed out.

Jocko turned to Samantha. "Well, what do you think?"

"No furniture damaged and no one taken to the ER, so I guess we can say it turned out good." A slight smile flickered on Samantha's face then disappeared.

Jocko put his hands in his pockets. "Kingpin is like a wounded bear and could do a lot of damage to this station if he decides to lawyer up. A court fight would hurt us as much as it would him, and he knows it. He's ruthless, desperate, and has a lot of resources. It would be a mistake to underestimate him. I'm not going to sleep well until this is over."

Samantha stared at Jocko. "Neither am I."

—⚊—

Whitherspoon staggered to the parking lot on wobbly legs. He got in his Porsche and drove toward the desert, running two red lights in the process. *Now I know why Jocko gave me Friday night off. He planned to fire me and wanted me out of the building after he did it.* As Whitherspoon's car sped through the desert, his thoughts raced even faster, until his cell phone rang.

"Hey, Kingpin, it's Leon. I just got off the phone with Fannie. We need to talk."

"I'm kinda busy right now."

"This'll only take a second. Fannie didn't get that job in Colorado after all, so she's still looking for employment. She's already used those contacts you gave her and wants you to send more."

"You did tell her we couldn't promise her a job, didn't you?"

"I did sorta. But she cut me off. She doesn't know how things work."

"Well, then explain how things work!"

"Yeah, sure. But if you don't get her a job, I'm afraid she'll go to Samantha and tell her everything about what we did to Pickler."

"Let her go to Samantha. I can't make anyone hire her, Leon. Would you give me a break?"

"Shit's gonna hit the fan...just sayin'."

Whitherspoon moaned. "I don't know what to tell you. Look, I gotta go. I'm getting another call."

"Hello, Tom?"

"Who's this?"

"Carmaletta."

"Oh, hi, Carmaletta. How're you doing? I'm sorry I didn't recognize your voice. I've got a lot on my mind right now."

"I've got something to celebrate."

"What is it?"

"Briggs Lake is hiring me to run their new women's shelter. I'll make a salary high enough to support us and will get a good benefits package. I'll have a flexible schedule so I can raise my boys properly and be here for them when they need me. I signed the contract today."

"Outstanding news, Carmaletta. Congratulations!"

"Now you can stop sending the monthly checks. I don't need them anymore. OK?"

"Sure. I'll stop sending them as soon as you get your first one from the city. It takes governments and companies forever to get their payroll set up. I've got lots of experience with this."

"Let's celebrate. The boys said you were off and might take them to a high school football game. I'm pulling rank on them. Instead, let me cook you all a nice steak dinner. What do you say?'"

"What time?"

"Six thirty."

"I'll be there."

Whitherspoon hung up and resumed his effort to process the fact that he'd just lost his job. He tapped a silent drumbeat on his steering wheel to accompany the thoughts marching through his brain as fast as the passing scenery.

What am I going to do about Fannie? I wish I hadn't trusted Rump to handle all the communications with her. I don't know for sure what he said to her. Now she's holding me hostage for his promises. I'm history anyway. Maybe I should tell Jocko and Samantha the whole thing. But wait—if I do that, I'll have to resign. There goes my career and my reputation. I better keep my mouth shut.

—⁓—

Whitherspoon arrived at Lake Francis in an hour, a trip that normally took an hour and a half. After parking the Porsche, he walked to a ceramic bench, shaded by a palm tree, with a good view of the lake. He retreated here for refuge years ago during his divorce. Staring at the lake in this calm setting had been the closest thing Whitherspoon ever came to praying—until the past few months.

He watched two brothers playing in the lake having a splash fight by scooping water up and flicking it at each other. It looked to Whitherspoon as if they were close in age and evenly matched. Neither seemed to dominate the other. *The younger brother is going to win this. He's the aggressive one. He's got way more intensity and fight in him than his bigger brother. Yeah, the little guy has the edge. I could always pick winners.*

"Do you think you're a winner?"

Whitherspoon recognized the voice, it was Eli. He turned around to see a young muscular lifeguard with shoulder-length blond hair standing behind him.

The lifeguard came around to the front of the bench and sat next to him. Whitherspoon's eyebrows moved down as he squinted. "How did you know what I was thinking? Are you a mind reader?" *The voice is Eli's, but he looks different.*

The lifeguard said, "I know you had an older brother who drowned when you were both swept away by a riptide. You saved yourself but couldn't save him and have felt guilty ever since."

Whitherspoon's jaw dropped. "Huh? Are you Eli or not?"

"You were a young child. Stop blaming yourself for not saving your older brother."

Whitherspoon rested his arm on top of the bench. "Since you know everything about me, you know I'm getting canned. Any ideas?"

"What do you think you should do?"

"I think I should sue them for everything they've got and ruin their reputation. What do you think?"

The young lifeguard got up and searched the ground for a stone until he found a flat one and skipped it on the lake's surface. They watched the rings expand and then he looked at Whitherspoon. "You know right from wrong."

The lifeguard vaporized along with the ripples in the lake.

Whitherspoon gulped for air. "You're a big help, Eli."

—⁓—

That night, Carmaletta fixed a steak dinner to celebrate her new job. Jamie and Jason were excited to have Whitherspoon join them for dinner. After dinner they all played a shortened version of Monopoly, which Whitherspoon won, telling Carmaletta, "Never let your kids win games. It's bad for them. Make them beat you."

After Carmaletta sent the boys upstairs to bed, she turned her attention on Whitherspoon. "Can you stay for a little coffee?"

"Sure. How can I say no to your coffee?"

"It might keep you up."

"I don't care. It's worth it. Bring it on."

They relocated to the living room, where she put on soft music. They placed their mugs on the coffee table and sat next to each other on the couch, their thighs touching. Carmaletta looked deeply into Whitherspoon's eyes. "If you don't mind, I think we should keep the TV off. You see enough of Briggs News 20 at work."

"Fine with me."

"I'm so happy to have this new job and to be able to share it with you."

"I'm glad you want to share it with me. You always make me feel right at home. In fact, I feel more comfortable in your home than I do in my own. Weird, isn't it?"

"Yeah. You're so weird, Tom." She made a face then smiled.

"I do need to tell you something, though," he said.

Her smile was replaced with a sudden expression of alarm. "What?"

"I've been thinking a lot about you, and I think it might be best if I stayed away for a while. You're a great person and all. But—"

"But what?"

"I don't want you to think I've taken your boys under my wing and helped you a little financially—you know—to take advantage of you."

"I don't think that at all. I just appreciate having you as a friend," she said.

"You're a widow with two sons to raise, and it's only natural that you might feel attracted to someone who represents stability and security."

"You mean someone like you?"

"Well, yes, someone like me. And I don't want you, or anyone else, to think I'm using you at a time when you're vulnerable."

"What are you saying?"

"I think I should stay away for a while."

"Tom, would you please do something for me?"

"Sure. What is it?"

"Shut up."

She pulled him to her and kissed his lips. After a few seconds of hesitation, he kissed her back and wrapped his arms around her waist tighter. He lowered her down on her back and continued kissing her cheeks and neck. She moaned softly and clung to him.

Chapter 20

KILLER REVEALED

"Shayne, I met with the prosecutor this morning and showed him our evidence. He's given us the go-ahead to make an arrest." Strollo gulped his coffee. "Since we're dealing with a prominent TV station employee, we'll have to carefully plan every element of the take down."

Shayne Mendoza clenched his fists. "Consider it done. I'll work out the details and get the guys in position. It feels good to be able to take this killer off the streets."

"Yeah, removing a monster like that from the community is one of the best parts about our jobs." He reached into his desk drawer for a bag of Cheetos. "This calls for a celebration. I have more bags if you want one."

"No thanks, Louie. Make sure you wash all the yellow crumbs off your mustache." He laughed. "It's not cool."

"Yeah. Good point." Strollo grinned. "Thanks for all your assistance."

"Glad I could help."

"See you later."

After Mendoza left, Strollo found his cell phone and speed-dialed number one. "Samantha, we need to talk."

—◊—

"The Good News Show" was nominated for a local Emmy and propelled Briggs News 20 to the number one spot in the ratings. Whitherspoon's idea succeeded beyond expectations, and he felt vindicated. Besides Whitherspoon, only Jocko, Samantha, and Carol knew whom the viewers had chosen as the winner of the "Good News Contest." As the station employees set up the studio, they had no idea they would witness some shocking events they would recall vividly for the rest of their lives.

When the big night arrived, Whitherspoon and Martin wore tuxedos to make the night even more special. Carol Lackey entered the studio as the floor director secured the mics to each news anchor. "Kingpin, our winners are out of makeup and in the greenroom. Another thing, we have visitors. They wanna know if they can watch the newscast from the studio."

"Sure. It won't bother me." Looking at his coanchor, he asked, "Rex, you OK with extra people in the studio?"

Martin didn't look up from reading a copy of the newscast script. "No problem, Carol."

She left and returned with three guys who looked a little rough around the edges. Carol reminded the visitors to remain silent until the end of the broadcast and ushered them to chairs in the back of the studio.

The floor director interrupted Carol. "We've got thirty seconds to show. Here we go." He held up his hand and folded each finger as he counted, "Five...four...three...two..." Then he pointed to Whitherspoon and said, "Go!"

"Briggs News 20 news starts now. Good evening, this is Thomas Whitherspoon."

The wide camera shot included Martin, who spoke next. "And I'm Rex Martin. Thanks for joining us."

The camera switched to a tight shot on Whitherspoon. "Tonight we'll announce the grand prize winner of 'The Good News Contest.' You won't want to miss this. We'll be right back after these words."

Whitherspoon knew he needed a good opening tease to hook the viewers, but to keep them watching, he needed to save the announcement for the end of the show. There had been no breaking news since rehearsal, so the newscast proceeded as planned. The coanchors took turns reading the news of the day: crimes, scandals, investigations, and community events. Erin and Ronnie did their thing, reporting on the weather and sports.

As Martin finished up the last block before the big announcement, Whitherspoon had some time to reflect: something wasn't right and he felt uneasy. He had told Jocko and Samantha he would work until the end of his contract and help produce the retrospective of his career to be aired on his last day of work. After leaving the station, he would look for a similar job in another state. Despite a growing resentment for Martin's betrayal, he had treated him as if nothing happened.

Whitherspoon thought about his strategy. *This is one giant game and I'm playing against backstabbers like Martin and idiots like Rump. Jocko's made his move and so has Samantha. Now they think they've got me. Thing is, they're all playing checkers...I'm playing chess...and it's my move. I'll end this game with a checkmate that none of them will see coming. I'll eliminate all this stress and pressure from my life and move on.*

Movement on the wall behind the studio cameras caught his eye. There was someone else in the studio, but unlike the three scruffy visitors, this hipster wore a two-button, dark suit and dress shirt without a tie. He sported a neat mustache and used product to style his medium-length hair straight back. His expression serious, his eyes bored through Whitherspoon like lasers. He leaned against a chess king nearly as tall as he was, his other hand rested in his pants pocket.

Before he could give any more thought to the man, it was Whitherspoon's turn to speak. "First, I would like to thank all the viewers who gave us tips on the positive happenings in Briggs Lake and who watched the show. You made Briggs News 20 the number one-rated news show. Now I'd like to bring on the set the grand prize winners, former Briggs News 20 anchor Carl Pickler and his wife, Marlene!"

The Picklers joined Whitherspoon and Martin at the desk, triggering a collective gasp from among the crew and producers, who then smiled and nodded to each other, showing their approval.

After shaking hands with the Picklers, Whitherspoon continued. "Carl and Marlene decided to help the families of Manuel Dominguez and Chico Escobar, the taxi drivers murdered at Lakeside Park. They created 'Project Hope' and inspired the Briggs Lake girls' high school softball team to participate in fund-raisers, car washes, bake sales, and a series of exhibition softball games."

Whitherspoon handed Marlene the prize-winning check for ten thousand dollars. She smiled and said, "Thank you. The girls did the work—we only helped organize things."

Martin nodded. "We know, but the girls felt you and Carl alone deserved the recognition tonight. They told us none of this would have happened without your leadership and support."

The camera shot focused on Whitherspoon's face. "Their website took in PayPal donations from across the United States, and they've raised more than a hundred thousand dollars in donations and pledges."

The director switched to a wide shot in time to show Marlene handing the check to her husband, who took a close look at it and smiled.

Martin leaned toward the Picklers." So, Carl, what are you going to do with the ten thousand dollars?"

"We've decided to give it to the girls. This should allow them to get new uniforms and provide their travel expenses to compete in softball tournaments—for a couple years anyway."

The show closed with a tight shot of Whitherspoon. "Congratulations again to the Picklers, grand prize winners of 'The Good News Contest.' We'll close the newscast with video highlights of their car wash crew in action. Good night, and remember you always 'Hear It Here First.'"

When the floor director yelled, "Clear!" the crew tore off their headsets and rushed the anchor desk to congratulate the Picklers. The three men who had watched the show from the studio jumped Martin, wrestled him to the ground, and handcuffed him. From a side door, Detective Strollo sprinted into the studio as the plain clothes cops pulled Martin to his feet.

Strollo got in his face. "Rex Martin, you're under arrest for the murders of Manuel Dominguez and Chico Escobar. You have the right to remain silent...." After reading him the Miranda warnings, he looked up at the shocked news anchor. "Get him outta here, boys."

The special police unit escorted Martin, who gave no further resistance, to a waiting squad car for transport to the local jail. The staff, technicians, and on-air talent in the studio were in shock. Their ecstatic chatter over Carl and Marlene's award, a few minutes prior, had turned into stunned silence. They couldn't believe their eyes—their popular news anchor and rising star was doing the perp walk.

Jocko and Samantha seized the moment to push their way to the center of the studio. Jocko looked around the room at the astonished faces. "I know this comes as a shock to you all about Rex. He'll have his day in court, and he'll get the opportunity to defend himself. In the meantime, please don't discuss this with anyone, and refer people to Samantha. We'll send out a press release tonight."

Shayne Mendoza led Leon Rump—handcuffed behind his back, his left eye swollen, and his nose bleeding—into the studio.

"He made the mistake of resisting arrest, so I had to do a little persuading. I read him his rights. He knows he's under arrest as an accomplice to murder and for resisting arrest. Do you want to talk to him?"

Strollo put his hand on Rump's shoulder. "Mr. Rump, we have circumstantial evidence linking you to the first murder. If you cooperate with us fully, I'll do everything I can to help you."

Rump nodded, his head down, looking at the floor. "I didn't do nothing."

Strollo nodded to Mendoza, and he led Rump out of the studio as the crew looked on in amazement.

Jocko raised his voice. "Listen up. You're not to discuss this with anyone. Finish taking down the set, get us ready for tomorrow, go home, and don't speak about this—especially to the news media. Samantha and I will need to meet with some folks. Carl and Marlene, Tom and Detective Strollo, please convene in my office immediately. Thanks for your attention everyone. Good night."

Samantha, Strollo, Whitherspoon, and the Picklers followed Jocko single file to his office and settled around the conference table.

"I can't believe it," Whitherspoon said to no one in particular. "I wouldn't have guessed Rex as the killer in a million years."

Jocko indicated the meeting was about to begin by rubbing the top of his head, a gesture that got everyone's attention. "Detective Strollo, would you take us through some of the facts of your investigation and bring everyone up to speed?"

"Sure. Thanks, Jocko. As you all know, we've worked for months to piece the clues together from the two Lakeside murders. The trail led to Rex Martin. The first bits of evidence we discovered included Briggs News 20 brochures at the Manuel Dominguez crime scene and a Briggs News pen where Chico Escobar was slain. The crime lab and national registry used the DNA from strands of Martin's hair and fingerprints from a water glass to match the DNA and prints found at both crime scenes. We tested others but got a match only on him."

Jocko said, "It's hard to believe. Rex seemed like a normal guy—a good guy. I'm usually a pretty good judge of character."

Strollo looked at Jocko. "Sociopaths can seem normal in every other way—one of the reasons they're difficult to catch. Except they have a compulsion to repeat their violent acts, and patterns emerge." Strollo ran his thumb and forefinger across his mustache as if to straighten it.

Strollo regarded Whitherspoon. "You're close to Leon Rump, Tom. Can you shed any light on his involvement with Martin? Could Rump be an accessory?"

"Well, I know he's Martin's uncle. You'll have to talk to Jocko about how he came to work here." He shot an angry look at Jocko.

Jocko grimaced. "Leon recommended him, but I thoroughly checked his references and vetted him the best I could. He came highly recommended from several sources. I guess he fooled all of us."

An image popped into Whitherspoon's mind: Carmaletta's angelic face, dark eyes, and long, wavy brown hair. He recalled their conversation about people changing and doing what's right. Then the lifeguard flashed in his mind. His face flushed and his heart pounded like a jackhammer. His hands were moist and shaking, and he felt perspiration streak down his back in multiple streams. *Well, Kingpin. It's your move.*

"There's something I have to tell you all. Leon Rump and I conspired against Carl. I thought he was gunning for my job, so we planted false rumors to get him fired. Rump wrote the poison-pen letter to Jocko at my direction, and I ended up rewriting it. The accusations against Pick were all lies."

Marlene cried out, "You son of a bitch!"

"I'm so sorry, Marlene. I wish I could take it all back." Whitherspoon's eyes pleaded for forgiveness.

"What an asshole!" Marlene huffed.

"Marlene, please." Samantha patted her arm. "What about Fannie Larsen's feedback?"

Whitherspoon sighed. "Leon and I bribed her to lie about Pick using the N-word."

Samantha breathed out slowly. She glanced at Jocko and then back at Whitherspoon. "That reminds me of a call I got this evening—"

"Not now, Samantha." Jocko held up his palm. "Tom, do you realize the implications of what you've said?"

"Yes, I do." Whitherspoon spoke quickly. "I resign my position with Briggs News 20 effective immediately." He thought to himself, *Checkmate!*

Everyone glared at Whitherspoon in numbed silence. The only sound came from the air-conditioning fan. After a few moments, Jocko turned to the Picklers. "I'm so sorry I got sucked in. Will you come back to the TV station as senior anchor, Carl? I'll get the board to give you a generous pay raise to go with the promotion. What do you say?"

"I have an application in at the high school to teach and coach—"

"Carl!" Marlene glared at her husband.

He looked at her and smiled. "But I think I'll withdraw it."

Marlene broke down sobbing. Samantha handed her a tissue from Jocko's credenza.

Pickler helped his wife to her feet. "If you'll excuse us, I need to get my bride home. It's been a long day for the blond bomber." He took her hand and led her out.

After the Picklers left Jocko's office, Whitherspoon continued to stare at the closed door, deep in thought.

Jocko pointed at Strollo. "Detective?"

"No. We're done for now."

"OK. Meeting's over. The arrest is going to spread like wildfire and go viral on the Internet. The competition will descend on us like hungry wolves. I'll get the weekend anchors to fill in until we can get Carl in place. I'm sure Erin and Ronnie can help out as well."

Samantha nodded. "You got it, boss. You're going to also have to find a replacement for Leon Rump."

"I got that covered. I'm sure I can get Lonnie Eastwick to come out of retirement to run engineering for a while. Lonnie had the job before Rump and has forgotten more about engineering than Rump will ever know." Jocko motioned toward the door. "Thanks. Now I need to speak with Tom alone, please."

Samantha and Strollo left.

Chapter 21

UNFINISHED BUSINESS

Whitherspoon spoke first. "I'll go back to my office and clear it out tonight. I'll cooperate with the investigation into my activities and anything you want to know about Leon Rump. I'm so sorry I let you down, Jocko."

Jocko nodded. "I welcome your cooperation. We'll go where the evidence takes us and see how it all plays out."

"I know."

Jocko squinted. "A lot of stuff must be spinning around inside your brain."

"Actually, I'm at peace. I can hold my head high and look myself in the mirror and like the man I see."

"For what it's worth, I thought you did a good job for us, and I'm sorry your career ends this way."

"It's all right. There is one favor I'd like to ask."

"Sure."

"Carol Lackey's meant the world to me. Truth is, she's my best friend and probably my only friend. She had nothing to do with this mess—"

"I'll take good care of Carol. Have her see me." Jocko scratched his head.

"Thanks, Jocko." Whitherspoon extended his hand.

"Bye, Kingpin." Jocko shook his hand while looking him right in the eye.

"You're not such a crusty old bastard after all." Whitherspoon smiled.

"Whoever said I was?" Jocko made a face.

As Whitherspoon walked down the hallway from Jocko's office for the last time, he stopped to say good-bye to Samantha. Her door was closed, so he knocked.

"Come in," Samantha said.

He opened the door to see her sitting at the conference table with Strollo. "Just wanted to say *adios*."

"Tom, I'll prepare your termination paperwork in the morning and give you a call to arrange for the return of company property. It took a big man to do what you did tonight."

"I honestly didn't think I had it in me," Whitherspoon mused.

"You did," she said. "At the end of the day, you did the right thing."

"See you guys later." Whitherspoon closed the door behind him.

Samantha beamed. "Congratulations, Mr. Strollo. You solved two homicides. Good job, sir."

"Thank you, Ms. Ayres. I couldn't have done it without you."

He tilted her chin upward with his fingertips and kissed her.

—⁂—

When he got to his office, Whitherspoon saw Carol and Erin waiting. They had been crying.

"What's the matter with you two? Lighten up. You'd think someone died." He leaned over and put his hand on Carol's shoulder when he saw the streaks of mascara that had rolled down her face like tiny black rivers.

"I feel so sorry for Rex. That poor guy wouldn't kill anyone," Carol said.

"This is all so disturbing," added Erin.

"Yeah. I know what you mean. I didn't see it coming. Say, Erin, would you excuse us?"

"Sure. See you guys tomorrow." She left.

Whitherspoon put his arm around Carol. "Jocko needs to see you. Would you mind going to his office?"

"When?"

"Right now. We can talk tomorrow about Rex and all that. Go." He motioned toward the door.

"OK, boss. Whatever you say. Good night." She exited the office.

He packed up a few personal items and put them in his attaché case. He stared at the contents for a few moments before closing it. Then he made a call. "Carmaletta, it's me."

"Hi, Tom. You were wonderful tonight. The boys and I watched the entire newscast, and I couldn't stop crying over what the Picklers and the girls have done for us. God is so good."

"Yeah. He sure is, and the Picklers are special people."

"You're special too, Tom. I wish you would let me tell people you've been sending us checks each month. You should've won 'The Good News Show' contest."

"I'm glad the money's helped. I didn't do it for recognition of any kind. Giving is its own reward. I did it out of love for you and the boys."

"I know, Tom. And we love you back."

"Say, about that talk we had...that people *can* change."

"Yes."

"I wanted you to know I can now look myself in the mirror... for all the right reasons."

"That's great, Tom."

"Wondering if you could brew a pot of your coffee. I could sure use a cup."

"Sure."

"One more thing. Will you make sure the boys are in bed? I need to talk to you about a bunch of things that wouldn't be good for them to hear."

"They're already in bed—sound asleep in fact. I was about to turn in myself. I'm in my flannel pajamas."

"That's fantastic."

"What's fantastic? That they're in bed or that I'm in my flannel pajamas?"

"Both."

She laughed. "You're so funny. Coffee's brewing. Hurry home."

"I'm on my way."

He hung up and looked around his office one last time. As he walked toward the door, he noticed his beauty shot was askew. He walked over to the frame to straighten it. After standing in front of it for a few moments, he thought, *What the hell. It's fine the way it is.*

Then he picked up his attaché case again, turned off the light, and left his office for the last time.

Chapter 22

CASE CLOSED

Strollo's cell phone rang, interrupting an embrace with Samantha. They hadn't spoken much since Whitherspoon stopped by her office to say good-bye, but they had done a lot of hugging and holding.

He grabbed his phone off her conference table. "Strollo." He listened to Shayne Mendoza on the other end and nodded. "OK. Thanks. Keep me posted. I'll get with you first thing in the morning."

"What?" Samantha asked.

"Rump told Shayne that Rex Martin's dad was a Mexican taxi driver and had physically abused him as a child. He disciplined him by poking him with a knife."

Samantha cringed.

"There's more," Strollo continued. "Martin's real name is Martinez he had it legally changed when he began his broadcasting career."

"Interesting. So Rex Martin, I mean Rex Martinez, is a Mexican. Then Rump is an accessory?"

"Not necessarily. He admitted Martin visited him before he got hired, and he had given him a tour of the station and some brochures. He couldn't remember if it was the first of April or not, but he says it could have been. He says he never made the connection that it had been the night of the first murder."

Samantha took a deep breath. "Do you believe that?"

"Could be true. Rump seems to be living in his own little world. We have no DNA evidence linking him to either death. Our evidence is circumstantial: he turned off the security cameras the night of the first murder and he helped get Martin the job here."

"Why would he recommend Martin in the first place?"

"Rump's sister is Martin's mother. It was a favor to her."

Samantha slapped her hand on the conference table. "I almost forgot to tell you. Fannie Larsen called me looking for Rump."

"Did you ask her if she had lied about Pickler?" Strollo put his hands in his pockets, eagerly awaiting her response.

"No. I didn't think of it at the time. Sorry. Rump hadn't been returning her calls, so she gave me a message she wanted delivered to him."

"And that was?'

"She's pregnant."

"Wow." Strollo looked out the window and burst out laughing.

"What's so funny about Fannie being pregnant?"

"If they decide to get married, her name will be Fannie Rump."

After doing her best to stifle a laugh that would not be controlled, Samantha laughed out loud until tears ran down her cheeks. "You're sick, that's all I can say, Strollo. You're a sick man."

"That's called 'cop humor,' you'll have to get used to it."

When she finally composed herself, she asked, "What about Martin? Did Shayne say anything about him?"

Strollo, still pleased with himself for making a joke that cracked her up, stopped smiling and in a sober tone said, "Shayne said for the most part Martin's been polite, except he seems to change personas and starts calling himself 'Drago.' When Martin is speaking as Drago, he's a totally different person. His answers are filled with profanity, and he's spitting on the floor."

"Gross. Sounds like Martin has multiple personality disorder," Ayers opined.

"Yeah. Shayne contacted our counterparts in New Mexico about the serial killer. They never caught the guy. It could be Martin. If so, he won a local Emmy for reporting on murders he committed."

She took a deep breath. "You can't make this stuff up, can you?"

Their eyes locked. He moved closer to Samantha and took both of her hands in his. "Hannah's gone for the night at an away softball game. How'd you like to meet my golden retriever, Kenzie, and let me prepare one of my wonderful microwave dinners topped with a bag of Cheetos? Then we could find an old movie to fall asleep to."

She smiled at Strollo and her eyes twinkled. "I accept, Detective Strollo. That's a grand idea and sounds like the perfect way to end a day like this."

—⁓—

A knock at his closed door startled Jocko. He had just hung up from a call to the chairman of the board of Briggs News to update him on the day's events. He opened it and saw Carol Lackey standing there.

"Carol...what can I do for you?"

"Kingpin said you wanted to meet with me—tonight."

He noticed she wore fresh makeup, and his nose tingled when he smelled her cologne. "Oh yeah, that's right. I did want to meet with you. Come on in." He gestured toward his conference table.

He joined her at the table. "You really did amazing work on 'The Good News Show,' and I think you're one of the main reasons it succeeded the way it did."

"It was Kingpin's brainstorm. I only carried out his idea."

"An idea is only a thought until someone takes action on it. You're a doer, Carol, and you've made Kingpin look good—correction, you've made all of us look good."

"Thanks, Jocko." The kind words entered her soul like a healing balm. She respected Jocko. He always seemed to be a tower of strength whenever turmoil hit the TV station. "Speaking of the Kingpin. I've always felt that *you* are the *real* Kingpin, not Tom. You run the show, you call the shots—so in my book—you're the Kingpin."

Jocko laughed. "That's our little secret. Real kingpins don't talk about it."

"I knew all along."

"Since it's time for a little honesty, I've always admired your work ethic and integrity. You really care about your job and the people you work with. And by the way, your green eyes really stand out with the business suit you're wearing tonight."

"I thought this would be a good night to wear it for the first time," she said. "Erin helped me pick it out for a special occasion."

"Quite a night, huh?"

"Yeah. I feel so bad for Rex. I hope he doesn't turn out to be the killer. He seemed so nice."

"No matter what happens with Rex, there's going to be a lot of changes at the station. I can't talk about all of them now, but I could share a couple of things with you."

"I understand. Keep in mind, I'm willing to help any way I can."

"You didn't have to say that, Carol. Your actions tell me that every day."

She blushed and her face took on an angelic glow, the way someone looks when appreciated by someone else. She thought Jocko's broad shoulders symbolized his strength and that, though his frame was bulky, he moved gracefully on his feet. "Thanks, Jocko. Means a lot coming from you. I've always wanted to ask you something. Did you play football? There's something athletic about you."

"Not football. I competed in track and field. The decathlon was my specialty. I've gone to hell since those days."

"I don't think so. You still look athletic and healthy to me."

"I'm an old bald dude desperate enough to appreciate any compliments I can get. So I say from the bottom of my heart, thank you."

She laughed.

"That reminds me." He pointed both forefingers at her. "You've also got a great sense of humor, and you're the only person I know who can make Kingpin laugh out loud—at himself."

"Someone had to keep him humble." She made a gesture of mocked arrogance.

"That's been part of your job description, but I'd like to change your duties to manager of programming. Your producing skills, attention to detail, and ability to work with these prima donnas around here make you the perfect fit."

"I can do that."

"You're someone I've always counted on and I guess I should have told you that before now."

"Better late than never. Thank you."

"If you don't have any other plans, let's go to Hoochy's and celebrate the success of 'The Good News Show' over a drink."

"I'd love to, Jocko."

Epilogue

COFFEE TIME

Whitherspoon ambled toward the front of the TV station. He knew the front door was locked at 5:00 p.m. every night, but he could get the security guard to let him out. The news and production teams entered and exited through a rear entrance; he didn't want to take the chance of running into anyone. The hallway was dark and quiet, and then something caught his eye at the far end. At first he thought something was on fire then he realized it was a man about seven feet tall his eyes were like silver coals, and his body radiated white light. He smiled and held a flaming white sword flicking sparks of white light, which fell to the floor and glowed.

"Eli?"

Whitherspoon, still gripping his attaché case, ran down the hall to meet up with the man. When he got to the lobby, the man had vanished. The only person he saw was a guard sitting at a desk watching monitors of security camera feeds from around the building.

"Good evening, sir." The guard straightened up in his chair. "May I help you?"

"I don't know you. Are you new?" Whitherspoon asked.

"Yes," the guard replied. "I'm new. I finished training and everything, but this is my first night alone on the job. I'm Jim Robertson. They call me Big Jim."

"Pleased to meet you, Big Jim. I'm Tom Whitherspoon. Did you see a tall guy dressed in white come this way? He had to come by here it's the only exit on this side of the building and I could have sworn—"

"Nope. Nobody has been in the lobby since I came on my shift. Not a soul."

Whitherspoon made a face. "Hmm. I could have sworn I saw a man walking this way."

Big Jim leaned forward on his desk. "Say, I watched the newscast from the TV in the lobby. What's all the brouhaha about—you know, with that contest winner?"

"We awarded ten thousand dollars to him and his wife for their nonprofit, 'Project Hope.' They won the prize for their community service—raising money for the families of two murder victims. It's a contest we ran in conjunction with 'The Good News Show.'"

"Yeah. That's what I figured. I didn't catch his name, though. Do you know him?"

"I know him well. His name's Carl Pickler. He's the senior news anchor here at Briggs News 20, but we all just call him the Kingpin."

The End

Made in the USA
Charleston, SC
09 May 2014